David sucked i... his hand over ... was against her skin. She gasped as they came into contact, and she heard his breath catch, too.

"Beautiful," he said roughly, and then, anchoring her head with his other hand, he lowered his mouth to hers and kissed her properly for the first time.

"Can we lose the light?" he said, and she realized he was still afraid of her reaction.

"No," she said, not knowing at all if it was the right thing to do, but just sure she wanted to see him, wanted him to see her, so there would be no secrets, nothing left to shock or surprise or disappoint. She lifted her hand and touched it to his heart. "I want to see you. I want to look into your eyes. I want to know it's you, and I want you to know it's me, warts and all."

Caroline Anderson has the mind of a butterfly. She's been a nurse, a secretary, a teacher, has run her own soft-furnishing business and is now settled on writing. She says, "I was looking for that elusive something. I finally realized it was variety, and now I have it in abundance. Every book brings new horizons and new friends, and in between books I have learned to be a juggler. My teacher husband, John, and I have two beautiful and talented daughters, Sarah and Hannah, umpteen pets and several acres of Suffolk that nature tries to reclaim every time we turn our backs!"

CAROLINE ANDERSON

The Single Mom and the Tycoon

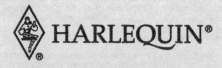

HARLEQUIN®

TORONTO • NEW YORK • LONDON
AMSTERDAM • PARIS • SYDNEY • HAMBURG
STOCKHOLM • ATHENS • TOKYO • MILAN • MADRID
PRAGUE • WARSAW • BUDAPEST • AUCKLAND

ISBN-13: 978-0-373-17546-8
ISBN-10:   0-373-17546-9

THE SINGLE MOM AND THE TYCOON

First North American Publication 2008.

The Single Mom
and the Tycoon

As part of Harlequin's 60th anniversary
celebrations, Harlequin Romance® is proud to
bring you a month of Diamond Brides in February.

There's twin trouble in Caroline Anderson's book
Two Little Miracles

PROLOGUE

Now what?

He turned his head, eyeing the vibrating, cheerful little phone on his bedside locker with distaste. God, he loathed that ring-tone. Why on earth hadn't he changed it?

It stopped, and he dropped his head back against the pillows and closed his eyes, trying to get back to that quiet place inside where nothing could reach him.

But not for long.

The phone rang again, and he sighed and picked it up.

Damn. Not Georgie. Anyone else—anyone who knew—but not his little sister. Not now.

Except she wouldn't give up, of course. She never did. She was going to keep on ringing and texting and driving him mad until eventually he gave up and spoke to her, so he might as well get it over with.

Bracing himself for the inevitable lecture, he stabbed the button and forced some enthusiasm into his voice. 'Georgie—hi! How're you doing?'

'Fine—not that you care, or you wouldn't screen my calls!'

His laugh cracked a little, and he coughed to cover it.

'Yeah, yeah, I know, I'm a lousy brother,' he said, not

bothering to deny the call screening. 'So—what have I done wrong this time?'

'Nothing.'

'Good God. A miracle.'

'Don't get overexcited, there's still a chance,' she warned, and he wondered what she wanted. Something, for sure. She always did. And he always failed her—

'Now, are you listening?' she went on. 'I've got to tell you something really important, and you've got to pay attention.'

'As if I don't always,' he said drily, and heard her chuckle.

'Yeah, right. When you're not ignoring me. I've been trying to get you for days to tell you—no surprises there. I don't know where you hide. Anyway, the thing is, Dad's getting married again—to Liz, Nick's mother—you know, my mother-in-law?'

'Married?' He straightened up, stunned. 'That's a bit sudden, isn't it?'

'Sudden? David, they've known each other for two years! It's hardly sudden, and he's lonely, and they get on so well. It's time he moved on. It's been seven years since Mum died. That's long enough.'

Seven years? Really? 'I can't believe that,' he said.

'Believe it. And you *have* to come home for the wedding. You haven't been home since before Dad's heart attack, and if it's not been one darned excuse it's been another, but you have to come home for this, no isn't an option. Your empire will have to take care of itself for a while. He wants you to be his best man, but he won't ask you himself, you know what he's like, but he really wants you here standing by his side. And don't even *think* about breaking something just to get out of it.'

'As if,' he said, trying to make a joke of it, but she wasn't laughing.

'Don't give me that. It's time you came home, David, even if you're in a total body cast,' she said firmly, and he swallowed again and stared down the bed at his feet.

He didn't think so. The timing couldn't have been worse—and, as for being his father's best man—*standing by him*—well, that was some kind of sick joke, wasn't it?

'When's the wedding?' he asked, hoping to God it wasn't another life-changing event he was going to miss because of this stupid, stupid—

'Not for a while. They want to get the spa finished so he can enjoy the wedding.'

'Spa?'

Her sigh spoke volumes, and he knew he was in trouble again. 'You really don't listen to anything, do you? Nick bought the old hotel at the top of the high street with Dan Hamilton and Harry Kavenagh: Dan's the architect, and Dad's firm are doing the work. Ring any bells?'

'Cheeky. Of course it rings bells,' he lied. 'Sorry, I've had a lot on my plate. I knew they were working on something, I'd just forgotten it was going to be a spa.'

'Not just any spa,' she said, and he could hear the pride in her voice. 'It's going to be amazing. They're turning it into a top-end residential and day spa and gym, properly state-of-the-art, and it's going to be fantastic but it's been a bit of a killer for Dad. It's a big job to oversee. It's due to open next Easter, and he says he can't think about the wedding till it's all signed off, so they want to get married as soon as it's open.'

Easter. He frowned at his feet, moved the left one, wriggled the toes. Winced as the pain shafted through it and, for once, he welcomed it. That would be some time in April. And it was June now. So—ten months. Would he be ready? Would he ever be ready?

Have to be. This was his father, and he'd asked for nothing over the past ten years. He'd lost his wife, had a heart attack and bypass surgery that David hadn't been able to be there for, ended up with crippling business problems because of his illness that he'd never once mentioned—and he'd gone through it all without asking his son for anything.

And he wasn't asking now, but David couldn't turn him down. Not this time. Georgie was right.

'I'll come,' he said. 'Tell him I'll be there.'

'Tell him yourself. Call him—if you really mean it.'

The door opened and a nurse came in with a porter and a big smile. 'We're ready for you, David.'

His heart lurched against his ribs and he held up his hand to stop her. 'I mean it. I'll come. I promise.'

'Really?'

'Really. Give him my love. I have to go, I've got a meeting now and I'm going to be out of reach for a little while, but I'll be in touch as soon as I'm back in range. Just tell him I'm coming.'

And without anything else, without saying goodbye or offering any further explanation, he turned off his phone, threw it into his locker and sucked in a lungful of air before meeting the nurse's warm, sympathetic eyes with the nearest thing to a smile that he could muster.

'Right, guys, let's get this show on the road.'

'You're sure? You do understand what's going to happen, David, and you're OK with it?'

No, he wasn't sure, not about anything, and he sure as hell wasn't OK with it, but he'd put this off for too long as it was. And he knew he didn't have a choice. Not if he was going to get on with his life.

'I'm sure,' he lied and, closing his eyes, he rested his head back on the pillow as she kicked the brakes off the bed and wheeled him down the corridor.

CHAPTER ONE

IT REALLY hadn't changed at all.

Bits were different. More houses on the outskirts, perhaps, and a new roundabout on the access road, but fundamentally the same. And it still felt like home.

Bizarre, when it hadn't been home for eleven years, and even more bizarre that, after more than three, he could drive back into the little seaside town and feel a wave of nostalgia that brought a lump to his throat the size of Ayers Rock.

He cruised slowly in on the main road in his little rental car, slowly absorbing the changes to the place where he'd honed his bad-boy skills and broken a hundred hearts.

Including those of his family, he thought with regret.

He hadn't meant to. He'd only gone to Australia for a gap year after he graduated, but somehow it had stretched on and on, and he'd ended up so entrenched over there with his business interests that coming home for more than a flying visit had become all but impossible.

He sighed. He'd always intended to programme in enough time to come for longer, but the road to hell and back was paved with his good intentions and, in any case, for the last three years the matter had been taken out of his hands. The accident had happened just a couple of days before his father's heart attack, and when he'd realised how serious his father's heart condition was he'd been gutted that he couldn't get home, but there'd been nothing he could do about it. He wasn't fit to fly, so he'd played down the seriousness of the accident and told them he'd broken his ankle.

Which was true. Sort of. Then he'd missed Georgie's wedding a couple of months later, as well—he'd been gutted about that, too, and she clearly hadn't believed that his ankle was still responsible—after all, how bad could a fracture be?—but there was nothing he'd been able to do about that either so he'd just made himself unavailable, deliberately turning his phone off so he couldn't be reached. After all, no news was supposed to be good news, wasn't it, and Georgie was used to him not answering her calls.

Better to let them believe he was indifferent than add to their worries. Or so he'd thought. Had he been wrong?

Still, he was here now, and it was time to face the music. He wasn't ready for this, but he was beginning to realise he'd never be ready, so he might just as well get on with it.

But not yet.

Putting off the evil moment a little longer, he headed towards the sea front, past the newly revamped hotel at the entrance to the town, smothered in flags advertising its imminent opening as the area's premier health spa and leisure club.

It was impressive. The last time he'd seen it, it had been a tatty, run-down dump of a place, clearly struggling and in need of a massive cash injection. It had obviously had exactly that and, as always, his father had done a good job, he thought with pride.

Swallowing that persistent lump in his throat, he carried on down the main street, expecting the same old shops selling the same old stock. Except many of the shops were new, he noticed in surprise—in fact it was looking lively and vibrant and really rather inviting in a quaint and quintessentially English way.

Sleepy old Yoxburgh was clearly thriving in his absence.

He dropped down the steep little road to the sea front, past pavements clustered with tables spilling out of the front of the pretty Victorian houses now turned into hotels and cafés and trendy sea front flats, and cruised slowly along the prom and up past his sister's house.

A big Victorian Italianate villa overlooking the sea front, it was part of a redevelopment his father had been involved in the last time he'd been home, and it made a stunning house. Impressive, yet welcoming at the same time. And expensive. Easily seven figures, if his finger was truly on the pulse of the UK property market.

The development had been the biggest thing his father had tackled to that point, but he'd applied the same principles of quality and integrity that he brought to everything and, yet again, he'd done a good job. At least until his heart attack, and then Georgie had taken over.

From what he could see at this distance, she hadn't let her father down. Unlike him.

He shut off that train of thought and drove up past the side of the property, studying the small cluster of top-end homes grouped around behind it. Nick had ditched the previous architect's plans and commissioned Georgie to redesign and finish the project, and she'd done a good job, at least on the outside. Again impressive, he thought, and yet homely. Well done, Georgie. He was looking forward to seeing it all in close up, especially the lovely house where she was now living with her husband and children. She'd told him enough about it and sent him photos, but it looked even better in the flesh.

She'd done well, but he'd never doubted she would, and if anyone deserved to be happy, it was Georgie. She'd had some rough times, got herself involved with a real bastard a few years ago, and it was great that she was happy now. But so many kids? Four and a half, at the last count. They must be nuts.

He suppressed a flicker of something that couldn't possibly be envy and drove round the corner towards his rather more modest childhood home, a solidly respectable, warm and homely three storey half-timbered Edwardian house full of nooks and crannies for a child to hide in. He knew. He'd spent his childhood hiding in them and infuriating his sister because she couldn't track him down.

He gave a hollow little laugh. Nothing different there, then.

He scanned the house and felt a pang of homesickness that took him by surprise.

It looked good. Freshly painted, the garden carefully tended, and his father, looking as solid and dependable as ever, was standing in the front garden with a slender, grey-haired woman who was smiling up at him with love in her eyes.

Not that he could see her eyes, but he hardly needed to. The body language said everything, but she wasn't his mother and it seemed—wrong?

'Don't be ridiculous,' he muttered, and kept right on past them, his heart thumping. Why shouldn't his father find happiness? Just because his own life had taken a sharp and rather vicious downward turn didn't mean his father didn't deserve to be happy.

Without thinking about it, he found himself driving out of town and down the winding lane through the golf course to the little community at the mouth of the river where he'd spent every available moment as a child.

Unlike the main town, the harbour hadn't changed a bit. Or had it?

Sailing boats were pulled up on the shingle bank beside the quay as always, and there were cars parked outside the pub beside the little green, but the Harbour Inn looked as if it had undergone a revamp, like many of the houses at the smarter end. Nothing drastic, just the subtle evidence of a little more cash injected into the neighbourhood.

The harbour was a bit of a Jekyll and Hyde, torn between the fishermen and the yachties, the pub marking the dividing line; the smart houses in their fresh new paint were clustered together at one end and at the other, down near the ferry slipway and the entrance to the boatyard, the higgledy-piggledy collection of old wooden bungalows and huts and sheds that made up the rest of the little community were clustered round the scruffy but bustling café that hadn't seen a coat of paint in years.

It had sold the best fish and chips in town, though, he remembered, and he'd bet it still did.

He parked the car on the quay—pay and display now, he noticed, and realised he didn't have a single coin of English money. Oh, what the hell. It was the end of April. Who was going to check on him?

But, just in case, he went over to the café, bought a cup of coffee in a foam cup and put the change in the meter, stuck the ticket in his windscreen and went for a wander while his coffee cooled.

And saw other changes. A new chandlery, some very expensive craft tied up to the moorings in the river, a new clubhouse for the yacht club—all sorts of changes, but the old ferry was still tied up to the jetty, and there was a pile of lobster pots and nets heaped against the fish shack. They were probably the same ones that had been there in his youth.

He turned a little sharply, and winced. God, his leg hurt after the flight. He stretched, flexed his knee, limping slightly as he reached the jetty and stood there, breathing in the familiar air.

'Davey?'

He turned his head, incredulous. 'Bob? Hell, you're still here?' he said with a laugh, and found himself engulfed in a hug that smelt of sweat and tar and bilge water, with more than a lingering trace of fish. It was the most welcome hug he'd had in years, and he blinked hard and stood back, studying the wrinkled, sun-trammelled face of the old harbour master, those shrewd eyes still brilliant blue and seeing altogether too much.

'They said you were coming home for the wedding. Your sister didn't believe it, but I knew you wouldn't let the old man down.' He jerked his head at David's feet. 'So what's this limp then?'

He shrugged and grinned. 'Nothing. A bit of bother with a propeller.'

Bob winced. 'Would have thought you'd know better than to do something daft like that,' he said gruffly.

David didn't bother to explain. Where to start? Or

end, more to the point. That was the hard bit. He looked around. 'Don't suppose there's anywhere round here to rent for a few weeks, is there? I don't fancy a hotel.'

'Not going home to stay? That'll hurt, Davey. He'll be expecting you.'

He shook his head at the old man. 'I need my space, Bob, and so does he. Anyway, he's got better things to do than entertain me.'

'If you say so.'

'I do.'

Bob nodded thoughtfully, then he jerked his head towards the posher end. 'You could try Molly Blythe. She takes paying guests sometimes. I don't know if she's up and running yet for the summer season, but it's worth a try. Up there—the little white place at the end— Thrift Cottage. Molly'll look after you if she can, and I know she can use the money right now. Just go and bang on the door. The kid'll be around if she isn't. I saw him heading back that way a little while ago. He's been crabbing off the jetty.'

Crabbing. Hell, he hadn't been crabbing in an English river for—well, for ever, and even the word was enough to bring the lump back to his throat.

He thanked Bob, drained the coffee and walked along the sea wall to the house Bob had pointed out, past the coastguard cottages and the little church, past the smart houses with the flashy cars, and, at the end of the cluster, set slightly apart from the others, was a pretty little white cottage set in a chaotic and colourful garden that looked as untended as the house.

There was a sign outside that said, 'Bed and Breakfast', but it was tired and peeling and faded with the sun. That didn't bode well, and he could see, now he was close up, that the sign was just a reflection of the rest of the property. The barge boards were flaking, the garden was overgrown and the rose on the front wall was toppling gently over into the shrubs beneath, taking the drainpipe with it.

Thrift Cottage, indeed. It didn't look as if anyone had spent anything on it for years, with the exception of the roof, which had new windows in it. Perhaps it was in the process of being done up—hence her need for money. He wondered what the neatly trimmed neighbours thought of Molly Blythe and her scruffy little house.

Not a lot, probably.

He went through the front gate that hung at a crazy angle on its tired hinges, walked up the steps to the door and rang the bell.

'The bell doesn't work. Who are you?'

He turned and studied the tow-haired, freckled child sitting cross-legged on the grass and studying him back with wide, innocent eyes. 'I'm David. Who are you?'

'Charlie. What do you want?'

His tone was simply curious, and David relaxed. 'I'm looking for somewhere to stay. Bob told me to come and find Molly—'

But he was up, legs no thicker than knotted rope flying as he pelted across the garden and shot round the corner. 'Mum!' he was yelling. 'Mum, there's a man. He wants to stay here!'

He reappeared a moment later.

'Mum's coming,' he said unnecessarily, because she was right behind him and looking flustered.

'Sorry, I didn't hear the bell—not that it works—I was gardening out the back. Well, more slash and burn, really. I was trying to find the shed so I could cut the grass. I'm Molly, by the way.' She grinned, scrubbed her hand on her equally grubby jeans and held it out.

He realised his jaw was about to sag, because that wide, ingenuous grin so like her son's had got him right in the gut, and he shut his mouth, collected himself and took her outstretched hand.

Somehow he wasn't in the least surprised at the strength of her hot and slightly gritty grip. She was tall, athletically built with curves in all the right places, and her smile, below green eyes as curious as her son's, was wide and genuine. She had a smattering of freckles across her nose just like Charlie's, and her auburn hair was scraped back into a ponytail. A wisp had escaped, blowing across her face and sticking on the fine sheen of moisture he could see on her skin, and he had a ridiculous urge to lift it away with his finger and tuck it behind her ear—

'I'm David,' he said, letting go of her hand and dragging his eyes back up from the low, slightly twisted V of her T-shirt. There was a leaf stuck in her cleavage, trapped against the soft swell of her breasts, and he felt the air temperature go up a notch.

Hell, maybe this wasn't a good idea after all, he thought a trifle desperately, trying to forget about that soft and enticing valley so he could concentrate on what she was saying.

'Um—Charlie said you were looking for a room?' she said, her voice, warm and slightly husky, lilting up at the end of her sentence. 'Are you on your own?'

'Yeah. It's just me. I need somewhere to stay.'

'How long for?'

'I don't know yet. A minimum of two weeks, at least.'

Her eyes widened. 'Oh, crumbs. Not just one night,

then. I was going to say no, but...' She swallowed and looked round a little wildly. 'Um—I'm not really organised yet. I've converted the attic this winter—well, I say I've converted—a builder did it, of course, but I ran out of money and it isn't finished yet so I haven't got anywhere to put you—how long for, did you say?'

He opened his mouth to say he'd changed his mind, but she lifted her hand to pull the errant strand of hair out of her eyes and her arm jostled that soft curve of flesh enticingly, dislodging the leaf and driving out the last fragment of his common sense.

'I don't know. At least two weeks. It could be a month or more,' he said, trying to tempt her into finding room for him, and hauled his eyes back to her face in time to see a flicker of hope mingled with desperation in those beautiful soft green eyes.

'Um—that's fine. Well, it could be. It's just—well, the house isn't really ready yet and the cabin—I mean it wouldn't take long, but in the meantime—I don't suppose you could find somewhere else for a night or two?'

And give her a chance to talk herself out of it? 'I'd rather not,' he said, cutting off that avenue of escape.

She chewed her lip and he almost groaned aloud.

'Well—I suppose you *could* use the cabin,' she said doubtfully. 'It's got its own little *en suite* shower room—the water pressure isn't fantastic but at least it's private. I've had guests in there for years but I hadn't intended to let it again until I've had time to decorate it, and I've been too busy... Oh, goodness, I don't want to turn you away, I really can't afford to, but...'

She trailed to a halt.

'So—is that a yes or a no?' he asked, tilting his head slightly and trying to keep the smile off his lips.

She hesitated for a second, then grinned again, and he felt something hot and dangerous uncoil inside him. 'That's a yes,' she said. 'If you don't mind roughing it a bit for the first few nights until the house is ready. The attic just needs a quick coat of paint before I can put you into it—maybe not even that, really. I won't charge you the full rate, of course—'

'Can I see it?'

'The attic?'

'No. The cabin.'

A flicker of panic ran over those incredibly expressive features, and he squashed another smile. He sincerely hoped she never played cards.

'Um—could you give me an hour? Just to sort it out a little. It hasn't been used yet this year—I hadn't got round to it because I wasn't going to use it for guests again until I'd painted it. I don't know if we can even get to the door.'

'I could help you.'

The panic on her face dithered and fought with common sense, and the common sense won. Her mouth curved up in a smile, she let out a sigh and her eyes filled with relief. 'If you don't mind, that would be great. I mean, it doesn't look anything, but it will, and it's really comfortable. I love it.'

Oh, hell. Molly was giving it the hard sell. She obviously needed the money badly and, even though alarm bells were ringing, the thought of walking away from her now was even more alarming. Unthinkable, even. He couldn't possibly let her down at this stage, no matter how grim the cabin was. And it was absolutely nothing to do with that enticing cleavage—

She led him round the corner and they came to a halt

in front of a tired but pretty timber building set on stilts
in the corner of the garden. She climbed the steps and
yanked open the door, pushing the overgrown rose out
of the way, and he followed her in, sniffing cautiously.
It had the woody smell of a beach hut, slightly musty
and reminiscent of his childhood, and light years away
from the luxury of his exclusive beach front lodge in
their retreat in the Daintree forest.

And if he had a grain of sense, he'd turn on his heel
and run.

'It doesn't look much, and obviously it needs airing
and a bit of a clean as well as a coat of paint, but it's
got gorgeous sea views and the bed's very comfortable. I don't charge a lot, and I do a mean breakfast.'

He obviously didn't have the necessary grain of
sense, because she was right. It didn't look much. But
it had its own bathroom, the views were glorious and
he didn't need luxury. Just peace.

'I'll take it,' he said.

Molly felt her shoulders sag with relief.

She'd been meaning to paint it for ages, but she
hadn't got round to doing anything about it because
she'd run out of money, and anyway people who wanted
accommodation early in the year were few and far
between so she hadn't felt pressured. Apart from the
weekend sailors, there weren't that many visitors, but
the time had dribbled by so she'd missed the window
for Easter bookings, and her chance of getting any solid
bookings now for the next few weeks was zilch.

So he was a godsend—not least because he was tall
and strong and fit and didn't seem to mind giving her a
hand with preparing it! Not to mention downright

gorgeous, but she wasn't going to think about that. About the lean, lazy grace of his movements, the neat hips lovingly snuggled by worn denim, the way the soft, battered leather jacket gave to the tug of his broad shoulders, those hard, warm hands with strong, straight fingers that looked capable and dependable…

He was running his fingers over the paintwork in the doorway, and she was busy fantasizing about how it would feel if he was running them over her when his thumbnail flicked at a little flake of white, pinging it off. 'It could certainly do with some work,' he said, and her heart sank, his gorgeousness forgotten as reality thrust itself back into the forefront. With knobs on.

'Tell me about it. The whole place could. I was going to do it but there never seem to be enough hours.'

He tipped his head, turned it, caught her eye. 'It wouldn't take long,' he said. 'Scrape it down, give it a coat of paint.'

'There are a million and one things that don't take long, and I have to do them all, starting with finishing the attic so I can put guests in there until I've done this.' She gave a tiny, only slightly hysterical laugh. 'Of course, in an ideal world I'd pay someone, but I can't afford to.'

'I could do it for you.'

She felt herself go still, and studied him warily. 'Why would you do that?'

He shrugged. 'Because I'm here for a while and I'll go crazy if I don't have anything to do but chat to the family? And I'll charge you.'

Damn. Always the bottom line. 'I can't afford—'

'An evening meal. Not every night. I'll be out sometimes, I'm sure, but most nights. Nothing flashy. Beans on toast, bangers and mash? And in return I'll help you out—paint things, do the garden, fix the guttering.'

'Guttering?'

He nodded. 'On the front of the house. The rose has pulled the downpipe off.'

'Oh.'

'But I can fix it. It'll only take ten minutes.'

'You can't do that,' she said, frowning at him as he turned towards her and filled the doorway, big and strong and capable. And very, very sexy—

'Why not?'

'Well—it isn't fair.'

'Why don't you let me be the judge of that? I can do it if I want—and I want. And I'll still pay you for bed and breakfast.'

'But I couldn't possibly let you—'

'Of course you could. If I work, you feed me. If I don't, you get to put your feet up. How does that sound?'

Wonderful. Blissful. Too good to be true. She eyed him warily and tried not to be distracted by the raw sex appeal that was nothing to do with anything.

'I can't afford the materials, and I don't have any tools.'

'Tools aren't a problem, I'll borrow my father's. He won't be needing them at the moment, he's got better things to do. And the amount of paint you'll need will be peanuts.'

She chewed her lip. He was right. It wouldn't take long and it wouldn't cost much. Feeding him would probably cost more, but if she didn't do something to repair and preserve the structure of the house and the cabin, she'd lose a valuable asset and a way of making money for good. And anyway, he had kind eyes. Sexy eyes. Gorgeous eyes, in fact.

'Done,' she said, and held out her hand to shake on it.

He shrugged away from the doorpost, took a step forward and his fingers, warm and firm and dry, closed around hers.

And after years of lying dormant, for the second time in the space of a few minutes her body leapt into life.

She all but snatched her hand back, shocked at her response, suddenly aware—oh, yes, so very, very aware!—of this big, vital man standing in her cabin, just feet away from her, radiating sexuality—and she was going to be sharing her space with him?

She must be insane.

She opened her mouth to tell him she'd changed her mind, but he stepped back, turned away and went out into the garden, and she felt the tension defuse. 'Where do you want this lot?' he asked, poking at a pile of prunings with his foot, and, following him out, she pointed to the shed.

'They have to go through the shredder but it's in there, and I can't get to it yet. Then they can go in the compost bin,' she told him. 'But leave it for now, I'll do it later.'

He turned back to her. 'I've got a better idea. I'll do it now, so you can get to the cabin. I'm sure Charlie here will give me a hand, won't you, Charlie? Then you can clean the cabin out and make the bed and start thinking about supper while I get my car from the car park and get settled in,' he said with another of those grins which would have been cheeky when he was Charlie's age but was now downright wicked, and with the grin came another surge of interest from her body.

Her mouth dry, she nodded, all the sensible things she could have said like *No*, and *I've changed my mind*, and *Go away*, all slithering out of reach as she headed for the house to collect her cleaning materials. Maybe an afternoon spent scrubbing the floor and walls and chasing out the spiders would settle her suddenly hyper-active hormones...

CHAPTER TWO

'So—DO you come from round here?'

Molly had waited as long as she could, but by the time she'd dragged the mattress out into the sunshine to air and cleaned the cabin and scrubbed the bathroom and he'd shredded the clippings and cut the grass and she'd put the kettle on, her patience had evaporated, driven out by the curiosity that her mother had always warned her would be the death of her.

He had the slightest suggestion of an accent, but nothing she could define. South African? Australian? She couldn't get a handle on it, because it was only the odd word, but the rest was straightforward English. She knew him from somewhere, she was sure she did, and yet she was also sure that if she'd ever seen him before, she couldn't possibly have forgotten.

So, yes, she was curious about him—avidly so—and now they were sitting out on the slightly dilapidated veranda at the back overlooking the river having a cup of tea while Charlie kicked a ball around the newly mown lawn, and she couldn't wait another minute.

So she asked him the rather inane and obviously nosy

question, and for a moment he didn't answer, but then he gave a soft sigh and said, 'Originally. A long time ago.'

'So what brings you back?' she prompted, and was rewarded with a fleeting, rather wry smile.

'My father's getting married again in a couple of weeks, and I haven't been home for a while. And my sister put the thumbscrews on a tad, so I thought, as I was here, I should stay for a bit. She's got married since I last saw her, and she's having another baby soon, and—well, I don't know, there's a lot of catching up to do.'

And then, of course, it dawned on her, and the little thing that had been niggling at her, that tiny bit of recognition, fell into place and she knew exactly who he was and why she had felt she recognised him, and she couldn't believe she hadn't worked it out before.

'You're David Cauldwell,' she said, and he went perfectly still for a second and then turned and met her eyes, his own, so obviously like his father's now she thought about it, wary as he studied her.

'That's right. You must know my sister.'

'Only indirectly. I know George better. Liz—your father's fiancée—is a friend of mine. She runs an art class and I help her out with it.'

'She's a teacher?'

'An artist—didn't you know?'

She thought he looked a touch uncomfortable, as if he knew he'd been shirking his responsibilities to his father. Well, it wasn't her place to point it out to him, and she had no sooner said the words than she wanted to call them back. 'Sorry. No reason why you should know,' she said quickly, but he shrugged.

'It rings a vague bell,' he said, but he looked away, unable or unwilling to meet her eyes. Guilt? 'There were—things happening in my life when they got engaged,' he went on quietly. 'I may not have been giving it the attention it deserved.'

She—just—stopped herself from asking what things had been happening that could have been so important that he couldn't give his father his time and attention. *None of your business*, she told herself, but she couldn't stop her mind from speculating. Woman trouble? He looked the sort of man who'd have woman trouble, but she'd bet it was the women who had the trouble and not him. He'd kiss them off with some gorgeous flowers and that wicked smile and drive off into the sunset with the next beautiful blonde.

And they'd all be blonde, she thought disgustedly. Never redheads. Never *ginger*.

The old insult from her childhood came back to haunt her, and she felt her chin lift even while she acknowledged that at least she wouldn't have to worry about him messing about with her emotions. He wouldn't be even slightly interested in a penniless widow from Yoxburgh, with a son in tow as the icing on the cake.

According to his father, he co-owned a small group of highly exclusive resort lodges and boutique hotels in Queensland and spent his free time diving and fishing and sailing.

Which would explain the white crow's-feet round his stunningly blue eyes, from screwing his eyes up against the sun.

And he'd be far too macho to use sunscreen, and she'd just bet that tan went all the way from top to toe without a break—

No! Stop it! Don't think about that! Just don't go there!

And then it dawned on her that David Cauldwell,

property developer and entrepreneur, owner of select little establishments that were listed as Small Luxury Hotels of the World, was staying in her house. Her cabin, in fact, years overdue for a coat of paint—a fact which had *not* escaped his notice—and she'd even made him help her get it ready.

She wanted to die.

'So—what about you?' he said.

'Me? What about me?' she asked, trying not to panic about the quality of the bed linen. There was nothing wrong with the bed linen, there wasn't—

'Why are you here? You're not a native—I would have known you, or I think I would have done. So you must have been imported in the last ten years or so. And I assume you're living here alone with Charlie, since you haven't mentioned anyone else and you're doing the garden by yourself, which implies you're not in a relationship, because it's usually the men that get to fight with the jungle,' he said with a wry grin. 'So I'm imagining you're divorced or separated or something.'

'Something,' she conceded.

He tilted his head and searched her eyes, and she felt curiously vulnerable, as if he could see right down inside her to the sad and lonely woman that she was.

'Something?'

'I'm a widow,' she admitted reluctantly. 'I moved here when my husband died.'

His lips parted as if he was going to speak, then pressed together briefly. 'I'm sorry. I just assumed—'

'That's OK. Everyone does. And, to be honest, it sort of suits me, really. There's something safe about a divorcée. A young widow's an infinitely scarier proposition. They all think I'm made of glass, that I'll break if they say anything harsh.'

'They?'

She shrugged. 'Everyone. Nobody knows what to say. And men are terrified. They all think I must be desperate. The black widow spider doesn't really give us a good press.'

'No.' He smiled wryly. 'I can understand people being scared. It's such a hell of a can of worms. People don't like worms. That's why—'

'Why?' she asked when he broke off, but he just gave a twisted smile and looked away. Not before she'd seen that the smile didn't reach his eyes, though, and for some reason she felt the need to prod a little harder. 'Why, for instance, you don't tell your family what's really going in your life and why you're avoiding them?' she suggested, and he frowned and stared down into his mug.

'I'm not avoiding them.'

'So why aren't you staying with them? God knows your sister's house is huge, and your father's house is big as well. I mean, between them they must have at least six spare bedrooms, and you're down here sleeping in a shed, for heaven's sake! And I know for a fact it's not because you can't afford a decent hotel, so why me and not them?'

'I live in a hotel. I didn't want to stay in a hotel, I wanted to stay in a family home.'

'So why mine and not theirs?'

'Why not?'

'That doesn't answer my question.'

'You noticed.'

She gave an exasperated little growl and rolled her

eyes. 'So if you aren't avoiding them, why won't you answer my question?'

'Are you always so nosy?'

'No. Sometimes I can be pushy, too.'

She waited, her breath held, and finally it came, the smile she'd been waiting for, and he let his breath out on a huff and turned to look at her with resignation in his eyes.

'You're just like Georgie,' he said mildly. 'Nosy, pushy, bossy, interfering, trying to fix everything for everybody.'

She gave a brittle laugh and stood up in a hurry, the unexpected wave of pain taking her by surprise. 'Oh, not me. I can't fix anything for anybody. I gave that up years ago when I had to throw the switch on my husband's life-support machine.'

And scooping up the cups, she turned and went back into the kitchen before her smile crumbled and he saw the tears welling in her eyes.

Damn.

Had that been his fault or hers?

He didn't know, and he had to stop himself from following her. He stood up slowly, arching his back and rolling his shoulders, stiff from the flight and from gardening, and Charlie looked up at him hopefully.

'Want to play football with me?' he asked, and the simple, innocent question hit him square in the gut and took his breath away.

'Sorry, mate,' he said with a grin he knew must be crooked. 'I'm rubbish at football. Anyway, I'm just going to give your mum a hand with the washing-up.'

And turning away from the disappointment in Charlie's eyes, he went into the kitchen and found Molly leaning over the sink, her hands rhythmically and methodically squeezing a cloth in a bowl of water. Squeeze, release, squeeze, release, squeeze—

'You could have played with him,' she said, and he could hear the catch in her voice. 'Or said you'd do it another time. Not just turn him down flat.'

He let his breath out in a slightly shaky sigh and met her disappointed eyes.

'I can't play football.'

'Of course you can. He's eight, for goodness' sake! Nobody's expecting you to be David Beckham! You could have just kicked a ball around with him for a minute—or are you too important?'

'Of course not,' he said and, steeling himself, he added, 'I can't play football any more because I'd probably fall over all the time. I've got an artificial leg.'

He heard the tap drip, heard the cloth as she dropped it back in the water. She stared at him, eyes shocked, looked down at his feet, back up at him, and hot colour flooded her face.

'Oh, David—I didn't—your father didn't say anything—'

'They don't know.'

Her hand flew up to cover her mouth, soapsuds and all, and her wide green eyes were filled with a million emotions. 'Don't—? Oh, David. Why not?'

He shrugged. 'My father had a heart attack just a few days after my accident. It didn't seem like a good time to tell him how bad it was.'

'So you've—what? Lied about it ever since?'

'Pretty much. And not really lied. I told them I broke it, which was sort of true. It was certainly broken. It was only amputated last year. That's why I don't know much about Liz. I was in hospital when they got engaged, about to have the surgery.'

She stared at him, then at his legs, then back up, eyes wide with horror. 'How on earth will you tell them?'

'I have no idea.'

She dropped her hand, grabbed a towel and scrubbed the suds off her face, dried her hands and then picked up the cloth again and started squeezing it again furiously under the water as if she could squeeze away all the hurt and pain and injustice in the world.

'Molly, it's OK,' he said softly. 'It's better than it was before.'

'I don't understand,' she said, her brow furrowing. 'How can it possibly be better?'

'Because it works now. I spent two years in and out of hospital with an external fixator and endless operations to repair my foot. They replaced part of my ankle joint, grafted blood vessels—but nothing worked and nothing took away the pain. So finally I gave in and had it amputated, and it was the best thing I've ever done. I can move on now—start living again.'

She nodded, and he watched her throat bob as she swallowed. 'So—when did this happen? And how?'

'Nearly three years ago, in May. I got tangled up with a propeller—'

She gasped, but he didn't elaborate. He really didn't want to go there. 'Anyway, I've had ten months, which is a good long while to practise walking, but football—well, I don't know, it's one of several things I haven't tried, but I can imagine it might be tricky, and I didn't want to have to explain things to Charlie without you knowing first and okaying it.'

She let go of the cloth and dried her hands, turning

back to him, her eyes tormented. 'I'm really sorry. I know that probably sounds empty and meaningless and I hate it when people say they're sorry when they find out about Robert, but I really am sorry. I've heard so much about you, and all of it seems to revolve around you being active. So it must have been—must be— really hard.'

He tried to smile. 'It was. Being inactive nearly drove me crazy. But it's better now. I can get about easily, and I can run if I'm careful and the ground's flat, and I can swim and dive and drive my car, and apparently I can do gardening, and, best of all, it doesn't hurt any more.' Well, not so much, at least, and he could deal with his phantoms.

Her eyes searched his, and she nodded and gave a faint smile. 'Good.'

'Just—'

She tipped her head on one side questioningly. 'Just…?'

'Don't tell them. My family. Please. Not before the wedding. I don't want to put a damper on it.'

She looked shocked. 'I wouldn't dream of it. It's not my leg to talk about—and I won't tell Charlie either, and I'd rather you didn't yet. He's good at secrets but I don't think it's healthy to expect youngsters to watch every word.'

He nodded. 'Sure. Thanks. I won't. I'll try and make sure he doesn't suspect anything if you could just back me up when I have to let him down with things like the football.'

'Of course.'

'Thanks.' He scrubbed his hand round the back of his neck and kneaded the muscles briefly. He ached all over, and his stump was feeling tight in the socket. He really needed to get his leg off and lie down, and, if he was incredibly lucky, he might be able to sleep.

'Look, I know it's early,' he said, 'but I'm bushed. I've been on the go for thirty-six hours and I could really do with an early night. I think I'll just turn in, if that's OK.'

A little frown flitted over her face. 'Are you sure? What about food?'

He shook his head, and the little frown came back.

'Can't I make you some toast or something first, at least? You've been working so hard.'

His stomach rumbled, and he grinned. 'Actually, toast would be lovely. Thanks. I'll go and sort my stuff out.'

She appeared in the cabin door behind him a few minutes later, a mug in one hand, a plate in the other. 'Where do you want this?'

'This' turned out to be tea and a toasted cheese sandwich, and it made his mouth water. 'Wow, that smells good,' he said, trying to remember when he'd last eaten anything that he'd wanted so much. Days ago. More. 'Just stick it on the side. I'll grab it in a second. Thanks.'

'My pleasure. Look, David, are you sure you'll be all right out here? I mean—what if you need something in the night? A drink or anything?'

'I'll get up,' he said, and watched her face scrunch up in a little scowl.

'Don't talk to me like an idiot child!' she reproved him. 'I'm just concerned about the steps.'

'I'll put my leg on.'

'Isn't that a fiddle?'

He laughed softly and straightened up from his suitcase. 'Yes, Molly, it's a fiddle. It's all a fiddle. Using crutches is a fiddle. Putting the leg on is a fiddle. Having to think before you get out of bed and fall flat on your face is a fiddle. But you get used to it. And I've had three years of not being able to get out of bed without thinking, so it's not a problem. Besides, there's water in the tap in the bathroom here if I need a drink. Now, if it's all the same to you, I'd like to crash.'

She recoiled as if he'd slapped her. 'Fine. We're going to get some fish Bob's saved for us and then I'll keep Charlie inside so he doesn't disturb you.'

She straightened up, backing off with a wounded look in her eyes that made him feel sick, but he was too tired and jet-lagged and generally hacked off to deal with it now, so he let her go, and, as she closed the door, he heard her call Charlie and take him away.

There was no sign of them when he emerged from his shower room a few minutes later after a brief wash that of necessity included giving his stump some attention—no question of just taking off his clothes and getting into bed like a normal person, he thought heavily as he laid his folding crutches down beside the bed within reach.

Oh, well, at least it didn't hurt any more—or not nearly as much. If only it had all been worth it, if there'd been any point in him having got himself into this mess, but his heroics hadn't been enough, in the end, and tragedy had had its way. It had all been a complete and total waste.

And he wasn't going to think about that now or he'd go stark, staring mad. Instead he'd think about Molly, and how she'd looked at him with those hurt, reproachful eyes when he'd bluntly dismissed her and all but told her to leave him alone.

Damn. He'd apologise tomorrow.

He got into bed and lay down in the bed with a sigh.

He felt disappointed, as if he'd let himself down somehow, and his heart ached with—what? Regret? Or just plain loneliness.

He rolled onto his front, jamming the pillow under the side of his head and stretching out his leg for the first time in what seemed like hours. Not that he'd been uncomfortable in the plane. Travelling business class was hardly roughing it, but it couldn't prevent the turbulence and he was exhausted, his body clock disrupted by the time difference. But that didn't mean he could sleep.

He shifted a little, and realised that the bed was, as Molly had said, very comfortable.

But not so comfortable that he could forget the look in her eyes as she'd backed away.

He thumped the pillow and turned his head the other way, and finally gave up and rolled on to his back, staring at the window. There was a chink in the curtains, and he could see the kitchen light on. She must be cooking their fish for supper, he thought, and felt a pang of regret that he'd bottled out. He stopped looking at it, turned his head away, tried not to think about what she and Charlie were doing and the fact that he could have been sitting with them and eating Bob's sea bass instead of lying there alone.

Then he wondered what time she'd go to bed, and where she slept and, exhausted though he was, he thought again of that revealing peep of cleavage he'd seen when she'd first come round the corner and introduced herself, and felt the heat coil in his gut.

Stupid. Crazy. He was jealous of a leaf, for goodness' sake!

Anyway, she wouldn't want him. Not now she knew. He'd seen the pity in her eyes, seen the look she'd given

his legs when he'd told her, the cringing embarrassment, the recoil.

He'd seen it before. Celia had looked at him like
that, the first time she'd seen his leg after the accident.

At least Molly hadn't been sick.

No. He wasn't going to surrender to self-pity. It was
a stupid, useless, destructive emotion and he had better
things to do with his life than wallow in misery because
the first woman in years to pique his interest was turned
off by his disability.

God, he hated that word.

Hated all of it.

Suddenly he didn't feel any older than Charlie, just
a kid again, who should have been running around with
skinny legs sticking out of his shorts, crabbing off the
jetty without a care in the world.

Where had it all gone?

And with a flash of insight, he wondered how his father
had felt, losing his son for the last eleven years. He'd
never intended to emigrate, but that was how it had ended
up. It hadn't been intentional, and he'd missed everyone,
but back home his father had missed him far more. He
knew that. Georgie had left him in no doubt about it.

And now he had to go and tell him that the son he'd
loved and missed for so long had come home *disabled*.

And he had to be his best man.

Hell.

He rolled on to his side, and saw an upstairs light on
now. Molly's?

Yes. He saw her reach up and close her curtains, and
the silhouette of her firm, lush curves made him ache
for something he would never have. Molly Blythe was
strictly off limits, a beautiful young woman who was

getting on with her life and who had better things to do than tangle with a man so physically and emotionally scarred he couldn't even tell his own father about the mess his life was in.

And, just to underline the stupid, crazy nature of this thing that had happened to him, his toes—the toes he didn't have any more—curled up in agonising cramp that made him whimper with the pain. Phantom limb pain? Nothing *phantom* about it.

He sat up and rubbed the stump, massaging it vigorously, trying to chase away the sensation, but it wouldn't go. He rummaged in his bag for the metallic mesh sock that seemed to help, and pulled it on, lying back to wait for the relief that usually came.

There was no pattern to the pain. Nothing he could tackle in one straightforward way, nothing that made any sense. Acupuncture helped, but he was a long way from his acupuncturist, so he lay there, retreated into himself and, by slowing his breathing and focusing on the sound of the sea in his head, he went to a place where nothing could hurt him, nothing could reach him.

Not even his phantoms.

It was a cry that woke her.

No. Not a cry. More of a shout, mumbled and indistinct. She got up and went to the window and looked out, listening, and there it was again.

And it was coming from the cabin.

Her heart thumping, she grabbed her dressing gown and ran downstairs, flicking the button on the kettle on her way, and went down to the garden, the grass wet against her feet as she crossed to the cabin and tapped on the door.

'David? Are you OK?'

He was mumbling something and, because she didn't know if he was ill or if it was just a nightmare, she opened the door and tiptoed in. 'David?'

Nothing, but she could see by the light through the gap in the curtains that he'd kicked the covers down to his knees and was twisting restlessly on the bed. He was naked except for a pair of snug jersey boxers, and there was a sheen on his skin, as if he was sweating. He was rambling, but as she stood there he said clearly, 'No! Don't let him die!'

He was dreaming—dreaming about something horrible and frightening, and without hesitating she crossed over to him and laid a hand firmly but gently against his shoulder. 'David!'

He stiffened, and then after a second his eyes opened, he stared at her, and then with a ragged groan, he dragged the quilt back up over his chest and covered his face with his hands, drawing them slowly down over the skin and hauling in a great deep breath.

He let it out, then sat up and propped himself up against the headboard.

'Sorry. Did I disturb you?'

'You were dreaming.'

He gave a harsh sigh and stabbed his fingers through his hair. 'Yeah. I sometimes yell a bit. Sorry.'

'That's OK. I did—for a while, after Robert died. The days were fine, but at night it would creep up on me. The dreams. Nightmares, really.'

She sat on the edge of the bed and looked at him. 'Fancy a cup of tea?'

'It's the middle of the night. You want to go back to bed.'

'Actually, I often get up for tea in the night,' she

admitted. 'I don't always sleep well, even now. It's no trouble—if you want one.'

His smile was a flash of white in the darkness. 'That would be really nice,' he said softly. 'I'll get up.'

'Isn't that a lot of effort? I could bring it here. Save you struggling with the steps.'

He gave a grunt. 'Just give me a minute,' he said. 'I'll come over. I'll be there before the kettle's boiled.'

Hardly, she thought, but she didn't say a word, just got up and went out, crossing the dew-soaked grass and running lightly up the steps to the veranda and then in through the back door. She saw the light come on in the cabin; then, as she was taking the teabags out of the mugs, he appeared at the top of the veranda steps, dressed in an open shirt, jeans and the shoes he'd had on the day before. And his leg, of course, which he'd had to put on, and was a fiddle.

She looked down at her feet, bare and wet with bits of new-mown grass stuck all over them, and wondered what it must be like never to walk barefoot, never to be able to wriggle your toes in the grass or the sand or the mud.

She'd die if she had to wear shoes all the time.

'Shall we go in the sitting room? It's chilly outside now,' she said as he came in through the door.

'You know what I really want to do?' he said softly. 'I want to sit on the sea wall and listen to the waves on the shingle.'

She eyed his bare chest through the open front of his shirt and tried not to get distracted. 'In which case you might need a bit more on. It's cold.'

'I'll be fine.'

'I think you've probably forgotten about the sea

breeze in Yoxburgh,' she said with a smile, and picking up the car rugs she'd turned out of the cabin earlier, she wriggled her feet into her flipflops, picked up her tea and headed for the door. 'Leave it open for Charlie,' she said, and went out, leaving him to follow.

She was right, it was cold, but it was lovely, too.

Tranquil.

Still and calm, with nothing to break the silence but the suck of the sea in the pebbles and the occasional clink of a halliard.

She handed him a rug, and he slung it round his shoulders and dangled his legs over the edge of the sea wall and breathed in the salty, fishy, river mud smell of the estuary mouth that took him straight back to his childhood.

'I love it here,' he said with a contented sigh. 'I've missed it.'

'Here?' she said incredulously. 'Really? Compared to coral islands and tropical seas and stunning reefs and all that sunshine?'

'It's not all it's cracked up to be. There's something about being cold, about falling leaves and bright, sharp frost and the brilliant green shoots of spring—and the birds here are different. Beautiful, subtle birdsong. The birds in Queensland are all raucous and colourful and loud, really, and some of them like the cassowary are downright dangerous. Don't get me wrong, they're beautiful, but there's nothing to beat a little brown wren or a chaffinch picking berries off a tree, and the dawn chorus here is so much more delicate.'

'You wait till the seagulls get up,' she said with a laugh. 'They're certainly raucous.'

He chuckled. 'I'll give you that. The gulls are always loud, wherever you are, but I love them.'

They fell silent, and for a long time she said nothing, but he could hear the cogs turning.

Then at last she spoke.

'Who died?' she asked softly.

He felt a shaft of dread. 'Died?'

'You said something in your sleep—it sounded like "Don't let him die" but it was a bit mumbled.'

He nearly told her. Nearly talked about it, but he didn't want to. Didn't want to get the whole tragic tale out and rake over the embers all over again.

Not tonight.

'I have no idea,' he lied and, twisting round, he lifted his legs up on to the sea wall, got to his feet with what could never have been called grace and picked up his mug and blanket.

'I'm turning in now. Thanks for the tea,' he said and, without waiting for her, he headed back to his cabin, shutting the door firmly behind him.

CHAPTER THREE

'GOOD morning.'

Molly tried for a smile. 'Morning,' she said, but her voice was strained, and David must have noticed because he gave her a keen look and sighed.

'Molly, it was just a dream. Forget it.'

'I can't forget it. There we were, sitting on the wall listening to the sea and just talking and I had to go and put my foot in it—oh, damn, I didn't mean that—'

He laughed. He actually laughed at her, to her horror and embarrassment, and then, before she could get her defences back in place, he took two strides across her kitchen and gathered her into his arms. 'Molly, stop it,' he murmured, and after a second or two, when it didn't seem as if he was going to let go or do anything stupid, she slid her arms round him and hung on.

Lord, it felt good. She hadn't held a man—not a young, healthy, vital man—for nearly seven years. And it felt good.

More than good. It felt *right*. She let her head settle down against his chest, so she could hear the steady, even beat of his heart, and gradually her own stopped thundering and she felt peace steal over her.

'I'm sorry,' she mumbled into his shirt, and his arms squeezed her and then let go, his big, warm hands on her shoulders easing her away so he could smile down at her.

'No, *I'm* sorry, I shouldn't have laughed at you. Come on, stop beating yourself up. I'm fine.'

'Will you tell me? Who it was?'

His hands dropped abruptly. 'One day,' he said, stepping back. 'Maybe.' He looked around hopefully. 'Right, where's that mean breakfast you promised me, or were you lying?' he asked, and her heart sank like a stone.

The look on her face was priceless.

Her hands flew up to cover her mouth, and her eyes widened helplessly. 'Oh! Oh, drat! I meant to go to the shops this morning first thing, but I overslept and then I remembered Charlie had holiday club, and I had to rush, and then I wanted to get back in case you woke up, and—'

'You forgot,' he added, trying not to laugh at her again.

She gave a guilty smile. 'Sorry. Apparently so.'

'Doesn't matter.'

'It does! And anyway, I was going to ask you what you usually have for breakfast. I meant to do that last night.'

'Fresh fruit, a croissant, coffee—nothing special.'

She nibbled her lip, and he had a sudden surge of heat, an urge that had nothing to do with breakfast or comforting her and everything to do with dragging her back into his arms and kissing her senseless.

Not that it would take long. She was so flustered right now she was pretty senseless already.

'Um—that's not my usual breakfast.'

'Well, give me your usual breakfast—or what you have of it in the house.'

Guilt flooded her face again. 'Well, that's the problem, really, because I can't. I haven't got any bacon or sausages or mushrooms or tomatoes—actually, that's a lie, I've got a tomato, but it's pretty wrinkled and you wouldn't want it. I didn't. And there aren't any hash browns or slices of black pudding in the freezer, either—'

The smile wouldn't stay locked in any longer, and he chuckled. 'So—having saved me from death by choles-terol, what do you have?'

'Eggs? Toast?'

'Done. Two boiled eggs—have you got two?' She nodded, and he went on, 'Lightly boiled, and soldiers. Can you do soldiers?'

She laughed, relief replacing the guilt in her eyes. 'I've got an eight-year-old boy. I can do dippy eggs with soldiers for England.'

'Excellent. And coffee?' he added hopefully, and her face fell again.

'Um—instant decaff?'

He rolled his eyes. 'What's your tea? Is that instant decaff?'

She laughed again. 'No, the tea's real—well, real tea bags. Is that OK? You haven't complained yet.'

He relented and smiled. 'Tea would be lovely. Thank you.'

And he sat down at the little table on the veranda, soaking up the chilly morning air and breathing in the familiar smell of the salt marshes while behind him in the kitchen he could hear her humming and pottering.

Then she appeared, with not two eggs but three, and a pile of hot buttered toast and two mugs of tea, and settled down beside him. 'You don't mind if I join you, do you?' she asked, and he couldn't help but smile at her uncertainty.

'Of course I don't. It's nice to have company.'

She went suddenly still, as if the idea was utterly novel, and then flashed him a smile. 'It is, isn't it?' she said softly, and pushed two eggs and a spoon towards him on a plate. 'Here, you'd better cut them open before they go hard. Dippy eggs are no good when they're hard.'

It wasn't only the dippy eggs that were in danger, he realised. That smile of hers had really got to him. He swung his legs round under the table and, as she winced and shifted, he realised he'd kicked her.

'Sorry,' he said. 'You're on the wrong side, really. The other side's a bit safer.'

She smiled. 'It's OK,' she said, but it wasn't, and it had reminded him in the nick of time why sitting there on the veranda with Molly having a cosy little breakfast was such a phenomenally lousy idea. Still, at least it had served one purpose, and it had been as effective as chucking a bucket of ice over him.

He shifted his legs to a safer distance, cut the tops off his eggs and concentrated on trying not to dribble yolk all down his chin.

'So—are you going to see your father today?'

He pushed his plate away and straightened up, staring out over the marshes into the distance, his face suddenly grim. 'I don't suppose I can put it off any longer, really.'

She didn't know why she did it—maybe because he'd made the first move and hugged her when she'd been distressed about upsetting him last night? Whatever—she reached out her hand and covered his and, after a startled second, he turned and met her eyes.

'He loves you, David,' she reminded him. 'He just wants to see you.'

He sighed softly. 'It's his wedding, Molly. His wedding and the opening of this health spa they've all done. It's a big moment for him, and I just want to be here for him without him having to worry about me. If he finds out—well, I just don't want him to. Not yet.'

'He won't.'

'You think he won't notice?'

'I didn't.'

'But you don't know me.'

She shrugged. 'No, but I know people. I know how they move, and I can tell if someone's limping or there's anything wrong, and I watched you in the garden yesterday and I didn't realise.'

'You watched me?' he asked, a flicker of something that could have been teasing in his eyes, and she felt her cheeks warm.

'Well—I *saw* you,' she corrected, and he smiled wryly.

'I prefer watched,' he said, and she realised he was flirting with her.

Only mildly, nothing heavy or dangerous or in any way reasonably responsible for the sudden rush in her pulse rate or the pooling of heat low down in her body in places that had been dormant for years.

She dragged her eyes away and went to retrieve her hand, but he'd turned his over and he had hold of her fingers, and as she pulled he gave them a little tug, so that she swayed towards him, and then, before she could react he dropped a kiss on her cheek and stood up.

'You're a good woman, Molly,' he said softly, and he went down the steps and across the garden to his cabin while she watched him, meaning to check for anything noticeably different about his gait and instead totally distracted by his easy grace, his body moving smoothly, strong and straight and solid, his shoulders muscular, his arms and legs long and lean, that soft, floppy mid-brown hair glinting with gold in the sun.

Her cheek tingled where his lips had touched it, and she lifted her hand and laid her fingertips over the spot, feeling the heat from his kiss warm her entire body.

She was still sitting there staring after him with her hand on her face when he came out of the cabin and looked up at her.

'What's wrong?'

She swallowed and felt her cheeks heat. 'Nothing. Sorry. I was miles away. So—what time do you think you'll be back?'

He shrugged. 'I don't know. I don't even know if Dad's around today. I'll go via the house, and then the site. He might be down there finishing off. Why?'

So I can be here for you, in case you need me after you've talked to him…

'No reason. I just didn't want you to come back and find I'd gone out. I could give you a key to the house,' she added doubtfully, wondering where on earth she'd put her spare, but he just shook his head.

'Don't worry about a key. I've got the key to the cabin, anyway. If Dad's not around, I'll try and find Georgie and, failing that, there's always Bob. I could go fishing with him. I'll see you later.'

'OK. I'll see you for supper if not before—or ring me.' She told him the number, and he keyed it into his mobile and gave her a grin.

'Right, I'm off.'

'Good luck,' she said impulsively, and his smile twisted with irony.

'Thanks.'

He slid the key into his pocket and with a little wave he walked round the side of the cabin and out of the back gate, his stride firm and even and steady.

No, she thought, you really couldn't tell, not when he was just moving around normally. Getting up off the sea wall last night had been a bit of an effort, but mostly—no, if he was careful, there was no reason why his family should find out until he chose to tell them.

And she couldn't sit there all day and wait for him to come back and tell her how it had gone.

Jumping to her feet, she cleared the breakfast things away, then went upstairs to her loft conversion and looked around. She'd promised him it would only take a few days to get it sorted but, before he could move in, she had to give it a really good clean and then get a coat of paint on the freshly plastered walls and ceiling.

She couldn't afford a carpet, but there was a rug in the cabin. She could bring that over, and it would cover most of the floor.

Still, first things first. She gazed blankly at the colour chart, and tried not to think about David and how he was getting on with his father.

It was ridiculous.

He had a business worth millions, with a turnover his competition would kill for. He was confident, competent and massively successful at everything he touched.

He didn't *ever* feel nervous.

But apparently he did today. His heart was pounding, his mouth was dry and he had no idea what he was going to say to his father.

Crazy. How about *Hello, Dad*?

If he was even in.

He wasn't.

At least, he hadn't answered the doorbell. So now what? Go to the spa and catch him in public at his workplace?

With a short sigh he turned away, just as a car pulled up on the drive and the woman he'd seen with his father the day before got out and came over to him.

'Hello, can I help you?' she said, her voice gentle and musical, and David eyed her, the woman who was to replace his mother, and struggled for words.

He didn't need them.

It took her about five seconds to work it out, and then her eyes filled with tears and she took the last few steps, arms outstretched.

'You came,' she said, as if she didn't quite believe it, and, without waiting for confirmation, she put her arms round him and he found himself engulfed in a warm, delicately scented and welcoming embrace.

And suddenly he could see what his father saw in her—the warmth, the genuine affection, the kindness. If Molly was a good woman, then so was Liz, and he was suddenly fiercely glad his father had found her.

He kissed her cheek, stepped back and smiled down at her. 'Hi,' he said. 'It's good to meet you. I've heard a lot about you.'

'Probably not as much as I've heard about you. Your father misses you, you know.'

'So I've been told.'

'Have you seen him yet? When did you fly in?'

'Yesterday—I arrived in the morning.'

Her eyes searched his face. 'So—did you stay in London overnight?'

He shook his head. 'No. I'm staying with Molly. I gather she's a friend of yours.'

'You know Molly Blythe?' she said, sounding astonished, and he shook his head again.

'No. I met her yesterday. She does B and B.'

'Yes, I know, but—David, you don't have to stay with Molly! Your father was expecting you to stay here. We've got the room ready—he'll be so disappointed.'

Damn. Yet again, he'd caused his father pain, and now he had to get out of it. 'I'm sorry. I didn't want to intrude on you—'

'Intrude? He's your father, David! And you won't intrude on me, I'm not living here yet.'

'Ah—I didn't realise,' he said, feeling himself colour slightly. 'Sorry. It's none of my business, but I just assumed—well, hell, you're adults. Why not?'

'Because of the grandchildren,' she replied simply. 'We didn't feel it was right to be together until we were married. So—no, we haven't lived together—but we are, as you say, adults,' she added with a smile. 'Enough said.'

Indeed. He filed that one away for later and dealt with the here and now. 'The trouble is I've promised Molly I'll stay there, now, and I can't let her down. She needs the money.'

'Well, that's certainly true.' She eyed him assessingly, then backed down, to his relief. 'OK. You obviously have your reasons, so I won't push, and I won't let the family push you, either, but if you change your mind—'

He nodded. 'Thanks.' The air lifted and he sucked in a breath and looked around. 'So—where will I find him?'

'Up at the spa. He's going through a snagging list with the site agent at the moment, then he and Nick are going back to Nick and Georgie's for lunch. I'm meeting them there in a little while. I was just dropping some things off. In fact,' she said with a glance at his shoulders, 'you can give me a hand to lift them, and then we'll go over there together. Some of the boxes are a bit heavy.'

And, opening the front door, she went back to the car and opened the boot. 'Here—could you start with this one? Goodness knows what's in it, it weighs a ton.'

He picked up the box, carried it in and yelled, 'Where to?' over his shoulder.

'Oh—upstairs,' she replied, and he carried it up and hesitated on the landing. Would they be in his parents' room? Oh, hell—

'In here,' she said, going into what had always been the spare bedroom, and he felt a tension he hadn't even been aware of ease a little. 'We've decided we'll use this room when we're married because of the view of the garden.'

He stacked the box beside the others, and followed her downstairs, her footsteps light except for a slight limp, a legacy from the accident which had killed her daughter.

'There's more!' she called and, with a wry smile, he went out to the drive to help her carry the rest of her things into what was to be her new home—the home she'd share with his father.

He had a sudden pang of envy, and for some inexplicable reason an image of Molly popped into his mind and caught him by surprise.

Not just Molly. Molly and himself. Together, eating dippy eggs on the veranda every morning for the rest of their lives. Now where had that come from?

He shifted the rest of the boxes while he pondered the idea and, when it was all done, Liz looked at her watch and said, 'Right. They'll be finished now and back at Nick's. Why don't you come with me?'

'Fine,' he said, and it was. The first hurdle was over, and the rest suddenly seemed much, much easier.

Till they got there.

'Ah. Everyone's here. I hadn't thought of that.'

Liz was standing by her car, eyeing the over-full drive with dismay.

'Everyone?' he asked.

'Harry and Daniel—and if they're here, their wives and children will be here too, probably. It'll be chaos. Do you want me to go in and get him?'

He thought about it for all of a second, then locked his car and found a smile. 'Just lead the way.'

She pushed the door open and went in, and he followed her down a beautiful entrance hall, past a graceful staircase and into a big, bustling family kitchen. There were children and dogs everywhere, and a little girl cannoned into him with a giggle and hid behind his legs.

'You can't get me!' she chanted, then ran off with the other children in hot pursuit, just as the adults turned and parted, and he looked across the room and met his father's eyes.

'David?'

The room fell instantly silent, with nothing to break it but the echo of the children's laughter as they ran away down the hall, and he could feel everyone's eyes on him.

'Hello, Dad,' he said quietly, and then with a strangled sound his father started towards him.

He met him halfway, crushed in a bear hug that brought a great lump to his throat, and then when his father released him Georgie was there, blooming with pregnancy, her eyes misting. 'Well, if it isn't the prodigal son. About bloody time,' she said, her voice cracking, and then she was in his arms, hugging him nearly as hard as his father had, her tiny solid body pressed up against him so he could feel the firm pressure of her bump against him.

His niece or nephew—her second child by a man he had yet to meet.

Hell.

She let him go and he looked around, recognising Harry and Dan and Emily, old friends from his teens, together with another woman who must be Iona, Dan's wife.

Not the quiet reunion with his family that he'd planned, but then the man he'd never seen except in photographs stepped forward, hand outstretched, and he felt the tension return.

'David—Nick Barron. It's good to meet you at last.'

'And you.'

The handshake lasted mere seconds, politely civil. No ice-breaking smile, no welcome, just a man in command of the situation who eyed him assessingly as he shook his hand. Oh, well, at least he hadn't crunched his knuckles, David thought. Much too civilised, but he guessed it was a thin veneer. The man had a core of steel. He had a bit of work to do there to repair the damage to his reputation, clearly. Ah, well. All in good time. He could deal with Nick. In his position he'd be just the same.

And then, in what seemed like a collective effort at damage limitation, they all started to talk at once, Dan and Harry breaking away to shake his hand with much more warmth, Emily reaching up to give him a kiss.

Someone put a glass in his hand, and then he was handed a sandwich, and his father put a hand on his arm and led him away, sitting him down at a table to one side and staring at him intently, relearning a face that time and circumstances had changed. He knew this. He was doing the self-same thing.

'You look…'

'Older?' he said with a wry smile at his father.

'Well—yes. More mature, anyway. I keep forgetting you've changed since you went away. You weren't much more than a boy then.'

'Yes, I was,' he corrected gently. 'You saw to that. And I was very grateful for it, and for all the other things you taught me. And it's not as if you haven't seen me since.'

'I know, but not enough. I've missed you, you know.'

He swallowed. 'I've missed you, too. I'm sorry I haven't been around since your heart attack.'

'No matter. You're here now. How's the ankle?'

'Fine,' he said truthfully. 'It doesn't give me any trouble now.' Unlike his conscience.

'Good. I'm glad. I'm sorry I couldn't get over to see you, it was obviously a bad break.'

He gave a choked laugh. 'Not as bad as your heart attack. I would have been here if I could. You do know that, don't you?'

'Of course I do,' he said, and he sounded almost convincing. 'So—how's it been? You've built yourself quite a little empire in the last eleven years. Has it been worth it?'

He thought of the last three, and blanked them out of his mind. 'Most of it. I've had my ups and downs—' to put it mildly, he thought '—but it's been interesting—*is* interesting.' And eye-wateringly successful, but that wasn't important now.

Clearly his father disagreed. 'I've kept an eye on your websites. You've done well.'

'You taught me well. And I listened.'

His father smiled. 'Good. I'm glad it's all come in handy. So—are you home for long this time?' he asked, trying and failing to keep the hope out of his voice, and David hated to take away that hope, but it wouldn't be fair to let him think he was home for good. That just wasn't realistic.

'A while,' he said, temporising. 'Several weeks, anyway.'

George's face fell. 'I suppose you can't take too long away from the business.'

If he only knew. David shrugged and tried for a smile. 'Oh, you know how it is. It all piles up when you turn your back on it. You can always come to me. I'd love to show you round.'

'We might. I'm thinking of retiring.'

'Good. About time. Just try and give me a few weeks' notice so I can clear the decks a bit. So—tell me about this leisure spa thing you've been doing. Georgie said it was wonderful and it certainly looks good from the outside, but I gather it's been a long haul.'

'It has, but we're just finished. The pool's commissioned, everything's been tested and signed off, and we've just done the final walk through, so at least it's come in on time and on budget.'

'That's a miracle,' David said wryly, and his father chuckled.

'Thank Nick. He runs a tight ship.'

I'll just bet, he thought, but said nothing, and his father went on, 'It opens on Thursday night. Big gala event, with lots of press and local dignitaries and celebrities and the movers and shakers of Suffolk. I don't suppose you'd like to come?'

'I'd love to,' he said, even though a fancy do like that was the last place on earth he'd choose to be.

'Really?'

He could see the pleasure something so small had given the older man, and the guilt redoubled. 'Really,' he said. 'It would be a privilege. I saw it on the way into town, and it looks fantastic.'

'Fancy a guided tour?' George said, and the eagerness on his father's face gave the guilt another nudge. 'They don't need us. It would be nice to have you to myself for a minute.'

He found a smile. 'Fine. I'll give you a lift, if you like? I expect your car's a bit hemmed in.'

They stood up, and Georgie came over and slipped her arm round David's waist, smiling up at him although her eyes were anxious. 'You're not running away?' she said, and he was stunned to see that she could almost believe it.

How much had his absence hurt these innocent people? He squeezed her back.

'No. We're going to see the spa.'

'Well, don't be too long. I want to introduce you to the children. They're dying to meet their Uncle David properly. Dad, you make sure you bring him back soon.'

'We won't be long. Tell Liz where we've gone.'

She walked them to the door and waved them off, and he led his father over to his hire car and opened the door for him, then went round and slid behind the wheel.

'Are you renting this?'

'Yes—well, I'm going to be here a while, and I'll need a car.'

'I've still got the Saab in the garage,' he said, and David paused with his hand on the key.

'Really? Mum's old convertible?'

His father smiled fondly. 'Well—she thought it was hers, but I drove it most of the time. I still go out in it now and then. I kept it for you.'

He felt a wave of emotion. 'I loved that car,' he said, a lump in his throat that no amount of swallowing would seem to shift.

'It's yours. It's taxed and insured—have it. It's automatic, but then so's this, so I imagine that's your preference anyway?'

'It is.' He nodded, giving an inward sigh of relief. 'I'll need to get rid of this, but I'm sure they've got an office somewhere nearby.'

'I'm sure they have. We can do it tomorrow, if you like? You can take this car back and I'll follow you in the Saab. Maybe we could go for a run in it.'

He shot his father a crooked grin and fired up the engine. 'That would be great. I'll buy you lunch.'

His father grinned back. 'Done. Just don't tell Liz what I have to eat!'

CHAPTER FOUR

'So how did it go?'

He smiled, a genuine smile that really seemed to come from the heart, and propped himself up against the worktop while Molly washed out her brushes. 'Great. Good. Much easier than I thought it would be.'

She gave him a keen look, searching his eyes. 'And did your father and sister give you hell for being away for so long?'

He gave a gruff laugh. 'No more than I deserved. And I met Liz. She's a star.'

Molly heard the warmth in his voice and smiled. 'I knew you'd like her.'

'Yeah, I do. She's not my mother, but she's not trying to be, and they get on really well. It was a real pleasure to see him so happy. And nobody said anything about my leg, so I guess it was a success all round.'

'Good. So, are you in for the night?' she asked, drying her hands and mentally pondering the void that was her fridge, and he nodded.

'If that's OK? They were all busy, and Dad was looking tired, so I left them to it. Is that a problem?'

She gave a little smile. 'It's fine. I need to go shopping, though, before I can feed us.'

'Want me to babysit Charlie?'

'Um—actually, I was wondering—I was going to give us pasta and pesto with a bit of grated cheese if you didn't come back, but I'm guessing you won't want that, and anyway Charlie had the cheese before he went to bed and I haven't got anything else in the fridge. I was hoping Bob would have some more fish, but he didn't and the fish kiosk was shut.' She ground to a halt, hating to ask him for money and not really knowing how to when the cabin was in such a state, and after all his help in the garden, but she'd bought the paint and when she'd gone back for more brushes, her card had been declined.

She should have bought the food first, but she hadn't realised how close to the bottom of the barrel she was.

So it was ask him or tell him she couldn't feed him.

She was just winding herself up to say the words when he pulled his wallet out of his pocket and withdrew a huge—*really* huge—wad of cash.

'Before you go, let me give you this. I don't know what you were going to charge me, but there's five hundred here, so I suppose it'll probably cover the first three weeks or so up front? We can work it out later on, but I didn't want you running short and having to nag me every few days. It'll save you having to use your card.'

She stared at it, hideously conscious of the prickle of tears behind her eyes. 'Um—are you sure? That's enough for—' She did a quick mental calculation. 'Gosh—it's well over a month. Weeks.'

'I don't think much of your maths.'

'There's nothing wrong with my maths!'

'Really? I would say there was, because either you

can't divide or you can't budget.' But his smile softened the words, and he held his hand out again, pushing the cash towards her until finally she reached out and took it.

'Are you sure you want to give me all this up front?' she asked. 'Since I can't budget?'

He grinned. 'Well, apart from the fact that I'd like breakfast in the morning, I thought it would give you a head start on the building materials. You'll need some paint for the cabin if I'm going to do it for you.'

'I've been meaning to talk to you about that,' she said, feeling the thickness of the wad of cash and resisting the urge to run away and kiss it. 'I started painting the attic room today.'

His mouth twitched. 'I thought you had paint in your hair.'

She laughed. 'Occupational hazard. I always have paint in my hair, only this time it's emulsion.'

'What is it usually?'

'Acrylic, mostly. I'm an artist—didn't I mention that?'

'You said something about helping Liz out in her classes, but I didn't really make the connection. So where do you paint?'

'In the little bedroom,' she said, wrinkling her nose. 'It's too small. I work messily, and I like to be able to stand back, so the only way I can do that is to go down the landing and then I'm looking into the light and—well, it just doesn't work. That's why I've done the attic. I'm going to move in there once I've done up the cabin so I can use it for guests again, then I can use the back bedroom which I'm in at the moment as a studio.'

'Except you've run out of funds and time.'

'Oh, you listened to that bit,' she teased, and his mouth quirked a little.

'I listened to everything you said,' he told her softly. 'I just didn't make sense of all of it at first, but I'm getting there. I'd like to see your paintings some time— later, maybe?'

'Sure. I ought to go shopping so I can feed you first, if you don't mind babysitting?'

'Not at all, but you aren't meant to be feeding me tonight. I haven't done anything.'

'But you did yesterday, and all you had was a sandwich, so I owe you.'

He hesitated, then smiled. 'OK. If you don't mind, that would be good. Where's Charlie? Did you say he'd gone to bed?'

She nodded. 'He's exhausted. He's had a really busy day at holiday club, and he's flat out. Why?'

'If it won't disturb him, I was going to have a look at the attic room while you're shopping—see what needs to be done so we can get you moved in there.'

'No, not me,' she said, shaking her head. 'If you're going to be here for a while, it would make sense if you had that room. It's got a little *en suite* shower room, and you can't sleep in the cabin while we paint it—if you really meant what you said...'

She trailed off, feeling suddenly awkward for mentioning the painting because he was frowning and she wondered if he'd had second thoughts or she'd simply stupidly misunderstood, but she hadn't, apparently, because he said softly, still frowning, 'That's your room. I couldn't take it from you. The paint won't worry me.'

She shrugged, relieved that he didn't seem to have taken offence at her reference to the painting and touched by his thoughtfulness. 'It doesn't matter. It's only short-term and, to be honest, without your money

I can't afford to do it anyway, so you might as well be in there because if you weren't here it wouldn't be finished anyway. And, as soon as we've finished the cabin, you can go back outside if you're still here and I can move all my stuff into my room and start painting again properly. I'm supposed to be having an exhibition soon, and there are a couple of galleries asking for my work and I hate to let them down.'

'Never a good idea, turning money away,' he agreed.

'Which is why I said yes to you yesterday,' she confessed ruefully, 'even though I'm not in the least bit prepared for having guests at the moment.'

He smiled. 'Oh, I don't know. The bed *is* really comfortable, the toasted cheese sandwich was excellent and you make great dippy eggs, even if it was the only thing on a rather limited menu. I'd give you—oh, nine out of ten? Maybe even nine and a half, bearing in mind the cup of tea in the night. That was above and beyond, really.'

She snorted. 'Either you're a shocking liar or your standards are too low. If you'd give me nine and a half with the décor in that state, what would you give your hotel?'

'Which one?'

'Of course, you're spoilt for choice. The most basic, then, to give me a bit of a chance.'

'The rainforest retreat? Twenty,' he said promptly, and then added, 'but I'm biased,' and laughed.

'And you have the nerve to criticise *my* maths,' she said with a chuckle, and pulled out a chair and sat down at the kitchen table, refusing to be insulted. 'So—give me a list of likes and dislikes, and I'll go shopping.'

He'd never been upstairs in her house, and it felt a little voyeuristic, but he had her blessing so after she'd gone he went upstairs to have a look at her loft conversion and see what else there was to do.

Not much.

She'd already done the ceiling and the first coat on the walls, so another good day and she'd be there. And it would be a lovely room. The window came down almost to the floor, and there was room on the wall opposite to put the bed so it would face the sea.

Not the beautiful turquoise tropical waters of the Reef that his room faced, but the cold, grey North Sea, sometimes flat calm, sometimes wild and tempestuous, ever-changing. And he loved it.

He stuck his head inside the shower room again. Small, but, like the one in the cabin, it had everything necessary. It wasn't a patch on his bathroom at home, but then his shower had a head the size of a dustbin lid and it was outside on a veranda with wooden slats for the floor and the rainforest for walls.

He went back into the bedroom and stared over the sea thoughtfully. He didn't want to move up here. It was Molly's room, and she ought to be in it. And in a perverse way he liked the cabin, for all the peeling paint and the shrub rose that scraped eerily against the walls in the wind. It had the same sea view, if from a slightly different perspective, and it was curiously cosy.

And a bit of paint wouldn't kill him.

He went down the steep, narrow stairs and paused on the landing. She'd said Charlie slept in the bedroom at the front, and he could see what was clearly a child's bedroom, the floor scattered with toys, the bedding bright and reminiscent of his own boyhood.

He put his head round the door and saw Charlie flat out on his back, mouth open, one foot hanging out of the side of the bed, and he smiled. Molly had said he was tired, and he certainly looked it. He'd sleep well tonight.

Resisting the somewhat unaccountable urge to tuck him in, he went back out on to the landing and hesitated. He could see her bedroom through the open door, the big high Victorian iron bed neatly made, the pillows topped with pretty cushions. Funny, he wouldn't have thought she was tidy, but apparently she was.

In there, at least. In the other room, the little room beside Charlie's, there was stuff everywhere—canvases, brushes, pots of dubious-coloured liquid with more brushes sticking out of them, piles of magazines and newspapers, tubes and tubs of paint, and the small patch of floor that was visible in the chaos was liberally splattered with blobs of vivid colour.

She'd trekked it out on to the landing too, in places, and he was amazed there wasn't more.

His curiosity overcoming him, he went in, picking his way carefully amongst the propped pictures and piles of magazines, and looked at the canvas on the easel, but it was barely started, just a wash of colour and a few scribbled notes pinned to the top of the easel. There were others stacked around the walls, none easily visible because of the clutter, and he didn't want to pry.

She was right about one thing, though. She needed more space. Desperately. There wasn't room to swing a mouse, never mind a cat, and how she managed to work in there was a total mystery to him.

Well, he could do something about that. He could help her finish the room upstairs, and then move her into it so she could have her bedroom as her studio and get on with working towards her exhibition.

Of course he'd lose the glimpse of her closing her

curtains at night, but so be it. There were bigger fish to fry, and he for one wasn't on Molly Blythe's menu.

More's the pity.

He turned to go back downstairs and caught sight of her room again, and his heart jammed to a halt.

Apparently she wasn't quite immaculately tidy. There was a pile of what looked like washing on the floor, and, mingled in with the T-shirt that had given him heart failure yesterday was a pretty lacy bra and a pair of matching knickers. Well, lacy string.

His gut clenched and he turned hastily away and went back downstairs before she came home and caught him lusting over a pile of washing, for heaven's sake. Lord, he was in a sorry state.

He would have changed into jog bottoms and trainers and gone for a run along the river wall to take his mind off it, but he was babysitting Charlie, so instead he made himself a cup of tea, in the absence of real coffee, and sat on the veranda and waited until she came home.

She wasn't long, and he helped her bring the things in from the car, then propped his hips against the worktop while she put everything away and tried not to think about what she might be wearing under her jeans and clingy little jumper. Unlike yesterday's T-shirt, the jumper didn't have a V neck, the scooped front hiding the little shadowed valley that had driven him insane yesterday, and so he could only speculate.

Or not.

'I had a look upstairs,' he said, trying to stick to the point. 'We should be able to knock that room on the head in a day. I'll get some tools from my father tomorrow and we can make a start on it when I get back after lunch. And then you can move in.'

She turned, hands on hips and more gorgeous than ever. 'But you're moving in up there! We've just had this argument!'

He shook his head, even more determined now he'd had time to think about it, not to give in. 'No. I can manage in the cabin. It's not like it's for long,' he reminded her. 'Besides, I like it. And it's your room, you should be in it. I can help you move all your stuff up there and you can have more space for your art. God knows you can certainly use it, what with your exhibition coming up.'

'Did you look at the stuff?'

'Your paintings? Not really. Just enough to tantalise.' Which went double for the underwear—

'Want to see?'

His mind screeched into overdrive. *Her paintings*, he realised after a second of fantasy run mad, and he nodded. 'I'd love to. Can we do it now?'

'Sure. I'll cook later, if you like.'

He followed her upstairs and stood in the doorway of the room while she foraged about and dragged canvases out of the corners and brought them out to the landing, propping them up against the end wall at the head of the stairs so he could get a proper look at them, and it brought him up short.

He studied the canvases in astonishment, her underwear forgotten, because they were stunning.

Powerful, vivid images, wonderful textures—bits of paper and photos stuck into them to create almost three-dimensional collages that built up one single image. Or maybe not.

It was like looking through a time-slip, shadowy images overlayed, as if each one had occurred in the same place but at a different time, and he was captivated. In one there was an old door in a crumbling wall. In another, trees in a forest. In another, the surf creaming on the shingle.

A series of those, in fact, he realised, big ones and little ones, with elements of the foreshore and the quay—part of her forthcoming exhibition?

'You're brilliant,' he said softly. 'Absolutely amazing. How much do they sell for?'

She shrugged. 'A few hundred at the most, the big ones.'

'Ridiculous. They're worth far more than that. You ought to get them into a London gallery.'

She laughed. 'I wish. There are some good galleries round here, though. One in Yoxburgh, a couple in Aldeburgh, some in Ipswich, Snape Maltings—there are lots of places. I do all right.'

'You're selling yourself short,' he told her firmly, and she shook her head.

'No. I'm selling. That's all that matters. I don't need fame, David. I need to earn a living. That's all. And I do that.'

He thought of the peeling cabin, the flaking paint on the bargeboards of the house, the broken gate, the outdated kitchen, and wondered what it was like to have such simple demands of life, and if it was because she'd lost the only thing apart from Charlie that mattered to her, and so nothing else was important any more.

And, because of that, he stopped arguing and went back downstairs while she tucked Charlie up, and he made a start on preparing the vegetables.

Then, while she was cooking—refusing his help because it was her job, not his, to cook—they chatted about nothing in particular and after they'd eaten he went to bed, alone and frustrated and torn between admiration of her artistic talent and wondering if he'd ever get the image of her underwear out of his mind...

'Wow! Cool car!'

David laughed and looked up at Charlie, who was standing teetering on the gate looking awed. Goodness knows why. He loved the Saab for all sorts of reasons, but cool it was not. His Mercedes, now...

'Fancy a drive?'

'Yeah! I'll have to ask Mum—'

'She can come, too.'

Charlie pelted off, legs flying, and came back a moment later with a grin. 'She's coming. She's getting my booster seat.'

'Great. Pile in, then.'

'Can I sit in the driving seat?'

'Sure.'

He got out and moved the seat forwards, and when Molly appeared her son was grasping the wheel and making revving noises. 'Look, Mum, I'm driving!' he said with a grin that cracked his face in two, and Molly laughed and leant over and hugged him.

Which gave David a perfect view of her sleek, rounded bottom, neatly encased in well-worn denim, and he had a sudden vision of those tiny little knickers and heat slammed through him.

No. Bad idea. Widow. Complicated. Back off.

But she was just so damn pretty, and she turned back to him and mouthed, 'Thank you,' and her eyes were soft and he wanted to wrap her hard against his chest and just cuddle her.

Ludicrous. When had he last wanted to cuddle a woman he wasn't related to? Dig his fingers into that taut, firm flesh and haul her up against him, sure, but *cuddle*?

Scary.

'Come on, pest, out of there,' he said, and Charlie scrambled over into the back and Molly piled into the front and scooped her hair up into a hairband and cobbled it in a knot while he shot the seat back and slid behind the wheel and tried very hard not to notice the shift and jostle of her breasts as she held her arms in the air and fiddled with her hair.

Thank God he was sitting down.

'Right—where to?'

'Oh! I don't know. Wherever,' she said with a smile that lit up the depths of her glorious green eyes. 'It's just such a gorgeous day and I love open-topped cars. Where did you get it?'

'It was my mother's. My father kept it for me.'

Her mouth made a perfect round O and she regarded him steadily for several seconds, the smile in her eyes replaced by sympathy and a tenderness that threatened to unravel him. 'That's lovely,' she said at last, and he smiled a little crookedly.

'I thought so.'

'Did you have a nice lunch with him?'

'Yeah, good. Oh, by the way, we put some tools in the boot too, so I can get started when we get back. OK, Charlie, where do you want to go?'

'All round the town,' he said, his bright eyes meeting David's in the rear-view mirror as he jiggled up and down.

'Round the town it is, then,' he said, so that was what they did. They drove back into Yoxburgh, past Georgie's house and along the prom, up through the town, past the spa with its flags and bunting, out on to the heath and home via the back roads along the river and through the golf course, with Charlie waving like royalty and giggling whenever anyone waved back.

Such a simple thing to give him so much pleasure, David thought, and then he looked at Molly and saw she was smiling too, her face tipped up to the afternoon sun, her eyes closed, and his gut clenched with the need to kiss her.

He really needed to get a grip.

'So, are you going to help me paint the walls?'

David frowned and laughed and shook his head. 'No. I'm going to fill the woodwork and sand it down and undercoat it. Charlie can help me, and you can do the walls if you promise not to splatter us.'

Molly felt her lips twitch, and he arched a brow. 'Don't even think about it,' he warned, and she laughed.

'As if I would. So, come on, then, where are these tools you said you'd got?'

He grunted and opened the boot of the car, unloading a wicked-looking power tool whose purpose she could only guess at. A saw? She shuddered with the images, glad to see it had guards all over it.

'I'll stash this in the cabin,' he said, and then came back and took out some more normal tools and filler and sandpaper. He shoved a couple of dust-sheets into her arms, picked up the other bits and pieces he'd sorted out and handed some to Charlie, and then chivvied her up the stairs.

'Right, first things first, we need tea, don't we, Charlie? Can't paint without tea,' he said with a grin, and so, dumping the dust-sheets, she went back downstairs and made the tea without a murmur, still slightly amazed that he was doing as he'd said. After all, why should he? He didn't know her, he owed her nothing—it was crazy.

And she was hugely, massively grateful.

By the time she got back upstairs with tea for them and juice for Charlie and a packet of biscuits, they'd spread out the dust-sheets and Charlie and David were bent over a piece of skirting board while he showed the boy how to fill the screw holes.

'A little bit in there, and stroke the knife over it gently—no, stroke, Charlie, not drag. That's better. Good. Right, do that one.' He watched, nodded and ruffled her son's hair affectionately. 'Brilliant. You'll be a painter yet. Right, teatime.'

'I've only done one,' Charlie protested, but he put the filling knife down when he saw the biscuits, and they ended up sitting on the floor in a row opposite the window and watching the sailing boats go by.

'I could look at it for hours,' she said softly, and he made a sound of agreement.

'I want to do more filling,' Charlie said. 'Unless I can have another biscuit?'

'No, because you won't eat your supper,' she told him, knowing full well he'd eat whatever she gave him because he was growing like a weed at the moment and ate everything in sight, but there was no way she was going to feed him rubbish and rot his teeth and he knew it, so he scrambled to his feet, picked up the filling knife and carried on, the tip of his tongue sticking out of the corner of his mouth like it always did when he was concentrating hard, and she felt such a surge of love it took her breath away.

'Thank you for being so patient with him,' she murmured, and David smiled.

'My pleasure. He's a good kid,' he said softly and, getting up, he went and joined Charlie, working alongside him. It was a little awkward for him doing the skirtings, she noted as she was getting her paint tray ready and sliding him surreptitious glances. He avoided kneeling on his left leg, presumably because it wasn't designed for it. Instead he knelt on his right and propped his left elbow on his left knee and worked like that, then, once he was sure Charlie was doing all right without supervision, he stood up and started work on the architrave around the doors and windows.

And that brought him closer to her. Was that the idea?

She didn't know, but he shot her a lazy, sexy grin and winked at her, and she felt her insides go funny. Bizarre, that a man who was a virtual stranger should turn her inside out with just a glance, but he could, and his presence turned a chore into something more like fun.

'I'm hungry,' Charlie said after an age, but he didn't look up and he carried on filling, so she put down her roller and stood back.

'How about I go and cook supper?' she suggested, but David had a better idea.

'How about we order pizza?'

Charlie looked up at that, eyes sparkling at his hero. 'Pizza? Mum, can we?' he begged, his eyes swivelling to her, the pleading in them unravelling her resolve.

This was getting tricky. She didn't let him have pizza usually, partly because of the cost and partly because of the lack of decent nutrition, and yet here was David, up there with the angels in Charlie's estimation, offering it without consulting her.

So what to do? Give in, and let Charlie have a treat, or refuse and cook something else and explain to David later?

Apparently her hesitation was enough.

'Charlie, could you be a star and run down to my car and see if I've left my phone in the pocket in the middle? You won't need the keys. Thanks, mate.'

'Mind your fingers,' she called as he ran down, and David turned to her as the thundering footsteps faded.

'OK, let's have it.'

'We don't do pizza.'

'Because?'

'Because it's expensive, nutritionally appalling and I don't want him getting used to junk food.'

He sighed. 'Sorry. I just thought—all kids eat pizza.'

'Charlie doesn't. Well, not very often, and not here. And, anyway, the deal was that I feed you.'

'I thought it would save you cooking,' he added. 'Give us more time to get this done.'

'I've got food in the fridge,' she said, feeling like a heel now and wondering if it was worth making such a fuss over. And of course the answer was no, but it was the principle, and he should have asked her in a different way—suggested it. Although, scrolling back through the conversation, that was exactly what he'd done, she realised, and she could quite easily have said something about food in the fridge and maybe another day.

And it would only be once, for goodness' sake!

Charlie erupted back into the room as only an eight-year-old could. 'It wasn't there. Do you think someone's stolen it?'

David looked down at her son, a rueful smile teasing his lips, and shook his head. 'No, I'm sorry, I've just found it in my pocket. Thanks for looking for me, though.'

'S'OK,' Charlie said and looked at her with those wide, appealing eyes. 'So can we get pizza now?'

She opened her mouth, caught David's shrug and smiled. 'Yes. Just this once, if David's treating us—but don't get any ideas!'

'I won't!' he said, and went back to his filling without a murmur.

'I'm sorry about the pizza.'

'Don't be. It was a really nice gesture. I'm just being silly.'

'No, you're not. He's your son, you're entitled to your rules. I didn't even think about it, and I should have done.'

'Well, you probably should, but family dynamics isn't exactly your strongest point, is it?'

'Ouch. That's not fair.'

'Isn't it?'

David sighed. 'Maybe a bit. I do screen Georgie's calls sometimes, but only because she nags. And since my accident it's been even harder. I hate lying to them. Avoiding them's easier.'

'Why didn't you just tell them?'

'When Dad had just had his heart attack? How?'

'Hmm. OK, I take your point.'

They were sitting on the floor again, drinking tea and staring out into the night. Charlie was in bed, the walls had had their second coat and Molly had brought up the tea as he'd finished off the woodwork. It was late, they'd been working for hours and he was ready to drop, but the room was taking shape and all that was left was cutting in the emulsion around the edges, and the top coat of the woodwork.

He couldn't believe how tired he was, and how satis-fied. He hadn't done anything hands-on like this for ages and getting back to brass tacks was curiously therapeutic.

Or it had been. And now Molly was getting at him.

'Tell me about your mother,' she said softly, out of the blue.

He shrugged, not really knowing where to start, not sure he wanted to discuss his mother with a woman who thought so little of his family skills. 'She was cheerful and homely and she cooked a lot. She was a good cook. And she worked hard. She ran the office side of the business for Dad, and she kept us all in order, and she never turned anyone away. She was a trooper.'

'You must miss her.'

'I do. I can't really believe she isn't still around.'

'That's because you've not been here. Maybe it's easier to pretend it's all still going on if you aren't face to face with it.'

Was that what he'd been doing? Pretending it was all OK? First his mother's illness and death, then his father's heart disease? More recently he'd thought he was protecting his family from the gruesome reality of his accident, but had he simply been refusing to face up to the hell his own life had become?

'I still miss Robert, even after nearly seven years,' Molly went on quietly. 'I expect I always will, just as Liz misses her husband, and your father misses your mother, but they're getting older, and they're both lonely, and she's a lovely woman.'

Like you, he thought immediately, and wondered about her still missing her husband after all this time. The thought was curiously unsettling.

'She is lovely. And I think Mum would have liked

her, which is a really odd thought. Did you realise they aren't living together till after the wedding?'

'Yes. Didn't you?'

He shook his head. 'No. I just assumed they were. I didn't think of the grandchildren, but then, as you said, family dynamics aren't my strongest point.'

Did he sound bitter? Maybe, because she reached out her hand and gave his fingers a little squeeze. 'I'm sorry,' she said. 'That was mean of me.'

'But maybe true.'

'So—where did you go for lunch?' she asked, changing the subject, and he felt his shoulders relax.

'Orford. We put the car in the car park and wandered along the river wall opposite Orford Ness. I didn't realise the old munitions testing station was now open to the public.'

'Yes, it has been for a while. The National Trust owns it. Charlie's been on a school trip.'

'Oh.'

'Oh?'

He shrugged. 'I wondered if Charlie would be interested in going. I thought we could take a picnic, but it doesn't matter,' he said, and then wondered what on earth he was thinking about, contemplating entertaining Molly's son, taking him on days out and picnics and so forth. Nuts.

'Maybe we can go somewhere else?' she suggested, and he made a non-committal noise and fell silent, and she didn't follow it up.

They sat there quietly for a while, then Molly turned to look at him. 'You look tired,' she said, studying him, and he smiled.

'It's a good tired,' he told her. 'A normal sort of tired,

from doing normal, everyday things. We had a long walk, and it's been a while since I did anything like decorating.'

'I guess it must have been. I suppose you've spent most of this year getting over your operation.'

He laughed. 'Actually, no. That was surprisingly easy. I've spent most of the year making up for all the time I had off and giving Cal a break. God knows I owed him. I've been working overtime on admin and dull stuff like that, and the only light relief has been taking the guests out to dive the reef.'

She rested her head back against the wall and turned to look at him. 'Tell me about the reef,' she said softly. 'Is it beautiful?'

He nodded slowly. 'Absolutely. There's something stunning about diving it, coming nose to nose with a shark or a giant potato cod or a manta ray, and the tiny little fish are just so striking. The colours are wonderful—I can't describe them. And it comes virtually up to the beach. You can't dive there, because of the crocs and the stingers, but you can see it from the glass-bottomed boat, and if you go out on the dive boat you can snorkel or scuba-dive on the outer reef. And the rainforest is fascinating. You'd love it. It comes right down to the water's edge there, and it's just amazing. But the diving's my favourite.' He swivelled to look at her. 'Can you swim?'

'Me? Yes, but I've never dived. Well, only off the side of a swimming pool.'

'You ought to come over—try it.'

She laughed softly, and he said, 'No, I mean it. You'd love it. You should bring Charlie and come over for a holiday.'

'With what, dear Liza?' she said incredulously. 'I think I'm doing well if I sell a painting before we run out of food. How on earth am I going to get us to Australia?'

'Easy. I'll pay for your flights,' he said without thinking, and she just looked at him and smiled ruefully and stood up, dusting herself off.

'I don't think so, David. Didn't you hear the pizza argument?'

'It's different.'

'You're damn right it's different. It's a whole different ball game, and I'm not playing. I'd love to see it, but if and when I do, it'll be under my own steam.'

He got to his feet, staring down into her eyes and wondering if there was any way he could persuade her, but from the look in her eyes he didn't think there was, and all he'd done by bringing it up was drive an even greater wedge between them.

He sighed softly. 'I've done it again, haven't I? Missed the point.'

'Yup.'

'I'm sorry. For what it's worth, I'd feel the same in your position.'

She smiled then, a proper smile, and, reaching up, she kissed him on the cheek. 'David, you'll never be in my position,' she murmured and, turning on her heel, she went downstairs and left him to switch off the lights and follow, kicking himself all the way while the imprint of her lips burned on his cheek…

CHAPTER FIVE

SHE shouldn't have been so hard on him last night, Molly thought. She was pretending to paint the window frame while she watched Charlie help David to wash the car on the drive behind the house, and frankly she wasn't getting a lot done.

She could just see them over the fence and, as she watched, David pointed to something on the bodywork, then squeezed a cloth out and wiped it, waited while Charlie did it, then tousled his hair and grinned at him. Teaching him how to do things. Treating him as his father would have treated him if he'd still been alive. And Charlie was lapping it up. She couldn't believe the difference he'd made to their lives in such a short time, and he was brilliant with the boy.

Still, he wasn't his own family, so maybe that made it all easier. Less complicated. Well, for him, anyway. It was going to get pretty complicated for Charlie when he went, she thought, and wondered if she should have a word with David about spending so much time with him.

No. Charlie would be back at school from Monday, and it was Thursday now, so his hero-worship would be naturally curtailed.

She sighed and dipped her brush again, trying to concentrate on something other than the man and boy outside the window. She wasn't getting on very fast, what with all the watching, but the room was nearly done. David had finished painting the woodwork this morning, all except the windows which were her job, if she could only concentrate.

The walls were now emulsioned a lovely muted duck egg blue, and the sloping ceilings were off-white, just to soften them. And it was looking lovely. She would have moved the furniture up here today, but she'd run out of time because tonight was the opening of the spa.

And he was taking her.

She felt a little flicker of panic, but told herself not to be so ridiculous. It was hardly a date. He didn't want anything like that to do with her. He'd been politeness itself and, except for that one occasion when he'd hugged her, he'd kept his distance.

Just as well, really, because Charlie was staying over at Georgie and Nick's with all the other kids tonight, and they'd arranged a babysitter to keep order so all the adults involved in the project could go to the opening and have a good time.

And they'd be alone.

She chewed her lip a little worriedly, and told herself not to be ridiculous. With all those glamorous women there, he wouldn't give her a second glance.

It was a black tie do, so it was bound to be a really dressy affair, and there was no way she could compete with Georgie and Emily and Iona in their designer clothes. Well, Iona was all right—she refused to surrender to pressure and bought clothes anywhere she felt was ethical.

Molly didn't even do that. She bought them where

she could afford them, and just hoped some poor child hadn't been responsible for making them. And that meant she didn't have a single thing to wear tonight that wasn't cheap rubbish or second-hand.

Apart from the dress Liz had bought her for the wedding next week, but that was only because she would be her matron of honour and she couldn't afford to buy her own.

The only other thing in her meagre wardrobe was a vintage beaded dress from the twenties that she'd bought for her first exhibition after Robert died, and she didn't know if she'd simply be laughed at if she wore it. She shrugged. Tough. Let them laugh. She loved the dress, and it hardly ever got an airing.

If she'd got the room finished so she could have advertised it and had more guests in, of course, she wouldn't have been in this position.

Except then you wouldn't have David, she reminded herself, and glanced back out of the window just as Charlie chucked a sponge full of water right into David's face.

She gasped and held her breath, then laughed till tears streamed down her face when David grabbed the bucket and hurled the contents at her delighted son. He ducked and ran, David hard on his heels and, just when she thought he was about to catch Charlie, he tripped over the verge and fell, rolling on to the grass and coming to an abrupt halt with his back up against a tree.

The laughter drained from her and, dropping the paintbrush, she ran downstairs and out of the gate, arriving just as he got to his feet, his hand on his side.

'Are you all right?'

He gave her a cock-eyed grin and breathed cautiously. 'I'll live, I think. It was the tree that got me.'

'Was that my fault?'

'No way, mate, I was just clumsy,' David reassured Charlie, ruffling his hair, and hobbled back to the gate, Charlie eyeing him worriedly as Molly tried not to hover and fuss.

'Charlie, could you pick the sponge and bucket up and bring them into the kitchen on your way to change into something dry?' she said and, while he was occupied, she turned to David and met his eyes.

'Are you really all right?'

'I'm fine,' he said, wincing as he lowered himself on to a chair on the veranda. 'Ouch.'

'I'm not surprised ouch. That was quite a whack you took against that tree,' she said worriedly. 'Let me see.'

He just raised an eyebrow, but he pulled his shirt out of the way to reveal a hard bluish bump slowly appearing on his ribs, and she winced.

'Stay there, I've got some arnica gel,' she told him.

'I'd rather have a cup of tea,' he murmured, so she put the kettle on and fetched the gel, and then had to try not to think about the warm, firm skin of his back as she smoothed it into his ribs. 'There,' she said, straightening up with a sigh of relief mingled with disappointment as he dropped his shirt down so she couldn't see that smooth, tanned, muscular back any more.

Get a grip, she told herself. This is a business arrangement.

But it didn't feel like one, not when he looked up and smiled his thanks and her body went into hyperdrive.

Thank God for Charlie, coming back into the kitchen in a fresh set of dry clothes, and for the car, which still needed finishing off.

'Pass on the tea, we'll crack on,' David said, getting

to his feet, and he went back to the car with Charlie, carrying the bucket of hot water and moving a little cautiously, and she went back upstairs to finish her window frame and try and get her thoughts back in order.

Or just watch him until she was sure he was all right.

'Mum's ready!'

David checked his bow-tie in the mirror, scooped up his DJ, opened the door of the cabin and stepped out, shutting it behind him.

Charlie was dancing from foot to foot, eyes alight. 'Mum's wearing a *dress*!' he said, as if it was the rarest thing, and David realised he'd never seen her in anything but jeans or jog bottoms. Not that four days really counted as never but, from the look on Charlie's face, it was clearly hugely significant.

Then he caught a movement out of the corner of his eye, and turned his head and stopped breathing.

Stopped breathing, stopped thinking, stopped everything except staring at Molly open-mouthed. She looked like a mermaid. The dress was incredible, beaded all over so that it clung to every curve and dip and swell of her body, shimmering blue and green in the light as she moved. And he wanted her.

'Does it look really stupid? It does, doesn't it? Totally inappropriate. I thought so. I'll go and change.'

He realised his jaw had dropped, and shut his mouth hastily. 'No!' He managed to make his legs work, and walked to the bottom of the steps, staring up at her incredulously and wondering how the hell he was going to keep his hands to himself all evening. 'You look—stunning. It's fabulous.'

She relaxed a bit. 'Really?'

'Oh, really. Really very fabulous.' He swallowed, and cleared his throat. 'Um—well, I suppose we'd better be off, then.'

'Charlie, get your bag,' she said, and Charlie shot past her and darted inside, leaving them alone. She nibbled her lip, drawing attention to the fact that she had lipstick on. Well, gloss, really. Shiny and slick and wet and— dear God, he wanted to kiss her. Kiss those soft, full, glossy lips until she screamed.

Damn.

'Does it really look all right? You're not just being polite?'

Polite? He nearly laughed out loud. There was absolutely nothing polite about the way his body was reacting, and he shifted the jacket to hide it. Although maybe she needed to see—

No!

'I'm not polite, Molly,' he said bluntly. 'It's not my style. I say what I think. And I think you look stunning.'

She blushed, her whole body softening, and he just wanted to haul her into his arms and hug her. Bad idea.

'I'm ready!' Charlie yelled, bouncing out on to the veranda beside his mother and grinning at her. 'Can we go?'

'Sure.'

She locked the door and walked down the steps to him, and he had a ridiculous urge to extend his arm to her, so she could tuck her hand into his elbow as they walked.

He didn't. He kept his jacket firmly in front of him and opened the gate instead and, as she walked past, he saw the split up the back for the first time and nearly went into meltdown.

* * *

Molly didn't really believe him about the dress.

Oh, she believed he liked it, but she wasn't sure it would be right for the evening. Suddenly, though, she realised she didn't care, because even if everyone else thought she looked silly, the look in his eyes couldn't be faked.

And he liked it.

More than liked it, she realised, glancing across at him just as he did the same and their eyes locked.

He smiled, a fleeting smile before he turned back to the road, but his eyes had burned with something very private that awoke the dormant woman in her, and she hugged it to her all the way to Georgie's house.

The boys erupted out of the house and dragged Charlie off with them. Georgie came out to greet them and her eyes widened. 'Molly! Oh, what a fabulous dress! Wherever did you get it?'

'London, years ago,' she said. 'On Camden market. There was a vintage clothes stall.'

Georgie touched it, felt the weight of it and sighed. 'Oh, it's beautiful. I'm so jealous, I look like a whale, but you look—well, you're far too good for my brother. I'll have to find someone who deserves you.'

She was laughing, but Molly didn't laugh, because the barb, however light-hearted, seemed harsh and un-deserved, and she wondered if his guardedness with his family was as one-sided as she'd imagined. In which case, she'd been even harder on him yesterday than she'd realised. She slipped her arm through his and moved closer. 'No way. He's mine,' she said with a smile, and his hand covered hers and squeezed.

'Shall we see you there?' he said to Georgie, and she could hear the reserve in his voice.

'Actually, I was hoping for a lift, but you've only got

the Saab. Do you want to come in my car? Nick's already there.'

'We can take you,' David said. 'You can squeeze in the back. You always used to.'

'I wasn't pregnant then.'

'I'll go in the back,' Molly said hastily and, hitching up her skirt, she flipped the passenger seat forwards and climbed in behind it to settle the argument.

The evening, as she'd predicted, was dressy, and amazingly she didn't look out of place. Nor did David.

Not out of place, but certainly, to her eyes, at least, he stood out from the crowd. Which, in such a glittering crowd, was quite an achievement.

Nick was there to greet them, standing in the grand entrance foyer by a beautiful old mahogany reception desk which had been lovingly restored. He kissed her cheek, shook David's hand and directed them towards the refreshments, and to Molly's relief Georgie promptly disappeared off to speak to someone and they were left alone.

The car journey had been short, because the house was only a few minutes away from the hotel, but it had given her a chance to watch him with Georgie, and she realised how much of himself he was holding back. With her, he was relaxed and chatty. With his sister, he was almost monosyllabic.

She'd thought it was just because of the tension between them, but in fact he was like that with everyone all evening, hardly relaxing at all, retreating into the background, watching his father with pride in his eyes and keeping close to her so she didn't feel alone, but distancing himself from the others.

Plenty of people recognised him and came over to talk to him, and his reaction was very revealing. He didn't seem to want to be drawn on what he was doing in Australia, and when person after person asked him how long he was staying, he was deliberately evasive.

Some even went so far as to tell him he was shirking his duty to his father and should have come home for good, and she could see by the tension in his jaw that he was hanging by a thread.

Only Harry Kavenagh didn't push him, just said, 'They've missed you, you know. We all have, but you have to do what's right for you.'

'I know.'

'It isn't always obvious. You'll work it out in the end.'

Like he had? Molly wondered. And Daniel? They'd both come home. Did Harry think that David would?

'We'll have to come and check out this retreat of yours that keeps you so busy you can't get home,' his wife Emily chipped in. 'It must be something really special.'

David gave probably one of his first proper smiles of the evening. 'It is. Just let me know when you're coming, and I'll make sure we've got space, although one of the other hotels might be better, with the kids. The retreat isn't really set up for young children.'

Of course not, Molly thought. It would be quiet and tranquil and romantic and there would be no place for a small boy having a water fight with his hero.

She frowned, wondering where on earth her thoughts were taking her and why, and tried to tune back into the conversation.

'Sounds like a really interesting set-up,' Harry was saying. 'You've done well.'

'Life's been kind,' he replied, and Molly thought of his leg and wondered how he could stand there in front of all these people, taking everything they threw at him and lying so convincingly that none of them realised the turmoil and agony he'd been through.

Tell them! she wanted to scream, but it was his business, not hers, and she knew he had another week and a bit to get through, not to mention the wedding itself, before he could let his guard down. Grief. The strain must be horrendous.

'Seen enough?' he asked after what seemed an interminable time and was probably only a couple of hours.

She smiled. 'Absolutely. It's fabulous, but social networking's never been my scene and I'll never be able to afford the membership, so it's all a little academic.'

'Shall we cut and run?'

'Good idea.'

His grin was infectious, and they sneaked out of the side door and headed for the car park with a mutual sigh of relief.

He chuckled and tucked her hand into his arm, covering it with his other hand as they walked across the car park. It was chilly now, and her little pashmina lookalike from the market was too thin to keep out the cold. She shivered, and he stopped.

'Here,' he said and, shrugging off his jacket, he dropped it round her shoulders, warm from his body. As she snuggled down inside it she caught a drift of his aftershave, warm and spicy and subtle, and even more subtle the undertones of his own special fragrance, and it was like being hugged by him. She breathed in his scent again and stifled a moan.

'Better?'

Oh, so much! 'Yes, thanks. Will you be all right without it?'

'I'm fine. It wasn't exactly cold in there.'

He opened the car door for her, helped her in and went round to his side. 'One down, one to go,' he said, and started the engine. 'And then I can escape.'

'Are you going back so soon?' she asked, shocked at how much that mattered, but he laughed.

'Oh, no. I meant escape from the public gaze and the interrogation of old acquaintances.'

'What about your friends?'

'What friends?'

'Dan and Harry and Emily.'

He shrugged. 'What about them? We've moved on, Molly. Our lives are all very different now, and mine's on the other side of the world. No point in stirring it all up.'

And maybe he'd felt that Harry was getting a bit too close, hinting rather too hard about him returning home. Why else would he describe his old friend's interest in his life as stirring it all up?

Such a private man. So much locked up inside him, and she was much too fascinated by all of it. By him.

And she wanted to know more.

Even if his life was, as he said, on the other side of the world. She felt drawn to him like a moth to a flame, and the fact that she knew she was going to get burned didn't seem to make any difference. Unable to help herself, she just flew closer.

'Are you hungry?' she asked, and he swivelled his head and grinned.

'Starving. Nibbles aren't my thing. I've never mastered the art of juggling a plate and a glass and a conversation.'

'Fancy chips?'

He laughed. 'Absolutely. Tell me where to go.'

'Down to the front and turn right. There's a place at the end near the roundabout.'

They cruised along, the lid down and the cool night air drifting around them, and he pulled up outside and ran in, emerging a minute later with two steaming bags of chips and a couple of wooden forks. 'I assume you wanted salt and vinegar?'

'Too right.'

He chuckled, handed her the bags and swung back out on to the prom, driving slowly along to the far end before pulling over and cutting the engine.

'Want to stay in the car or walk?'

'Walk,' she said and, handing him back the chips, she slipped off her shoes and reached for the handle.

He was there before her, holding the door open and taking her elbow to help her out, which brought her up against him as she straightened.

And then the atmosphere between them, already electric, changed and shifted, and she felt the world tilt and slide, never to be the same again.

She heard the soft hiss of air as he sucked in his breath, and their eyes clashed and locked. She could feel his body, warm and hard and very male, against hers, and where she'd lifted her hand to his chest to steady herself she could feel the steady thud of his heart behind his ribs.

Ignoring common sense, the public place, the bags of chips in his free hand, she slid her palm down and round, flattening it against his spine and easing him closer as she lifted her mouth to his.

His breath sighed out against her lips, and then he lowered his head that last tiny fraction and brought his mouth into contact with hers.

Just for a moment. Just for long enough for her to know that no one kiss could ever put out the fire in her blood, that no single touch would ever satisfy her, because when it ended there would always be another need, another time when she would have to hold him.

This wasn't going to burn out.

This was for ever.

The thought should have terrified her, but it didn't. She'd loved Robert. She'd loved him and lost him, and she could love and lose again, because there was no way she was going to miss out on loving this man just because he was going back to the other side of the world to a place where there was no room for her son in the adult-only world that was his home.

She knew it wasn't for ever. She knew it couldn't last.

He knew it too, knew he'd be going, but she wasn't going to let him run away without exploring this beautiful thing that was happening to them.

So she eased away and looked up into his eyes, saw the raw hunger in them and lifted her hand to cradle his jaw.

'Take me home,' she said softly.

She heard the catch of his breath, the sharp hiss of air as he straightened and stepped back, heard the chips hit the ground as he went round to the other side of the car and slid behind the wheel, firing up the engine as she struggled to fasten her seat belt with fingers that somehow didn't seem quite steady.

He stopped outside a pub, ran in and came back a few moments later and tossed something into her lap.

She looked down at the little packet and stifled a spurt of hysterical laughter.

Thank goodness one of them had some common sense.

He leant across and gave her a quick, hard kiss, then, straightening up, he snapped on his seat belt, fired up the engine and shot out on to the road with scant regard for the speed limit.

She could see his jaw working, see the tension in his face and hands, the fingers curled tightly round the wheel, and she knew his control was hanging by a thread.

That made two of them, she thought, and wondered if they'd make it home before one of them snapped.

His hand reached out, palm upturned on her thigh, and she slid her hand into it and hung on.

Not long now, she told herself. Not long and you can hold him, touch him.

Love him.

They made it as far as the cabin, then he stopped and stared down at her, his eyes dark in the soft light from the bedside lamp.

'I'm going to apologise in advance,' he said, his voice uneven. 'It's—uh—it's been a while. You remember the football thing with Charlie? I said it was one of the things I hadn't tried yet?'

She nodded.

'Well, this is another,' he confessed. 'I haven't done this—haven't had a date, haven't gone out, haven't made love to anyone since I lost my leg. Well, earlier, really. Years. Not since the accident.'

She felt a wave of tenderness towards him, and cradled his jaw in her hand, loving the rough silk of his skin, the stubble just grazing her palm as she smiled up at him and said a little unsteadily, 'Welcome to the club. I haven't made love to anyone since I lost my husband.'

He stepped back, his face a study of conflicting emotions. 'Hell, Molly—'

'Don't.' She reached out to him. 'Don't make excuses to run away from this. Don't stop now, please, David. I need you.'

For a moment he stood there, chest heaving, and then, with a muffled groan, he dragged her into his arms and crushed her against his chest. 'I can't stop. God help me, I can't stop, Molly, because I need you, too, and I know this is the wrong thing to do but—'

'No.'

'No?'

'No, it's not the wrong thing to do. It's the right thing. The only thing. It's our time, David, and I know it's not for ever, but let's just take what it has to offer and enjoy it—starting now.'

He couldn't believe it.

Couldn't believe that this wonderful, beautiful, sexy woman wanted him. Couldn't believe he was going to get to touch her, to hold her, to bury himself in the magical, incredible warmth that was Molly. Assuming he got that chance, and that once he'd taken his leg off she wouldn't recoil in disgust.

He stepped back again, finding the self-control from somewhere to make space between them. Actually it wasn't that hard. Suddenly aware of what he was about to do, his previously robust self-confidence deserted him and he turned away, his heart racing.

'I'm sorry, I can't do this,' he said gruffly and, walking out of the door, he crossed the garden, went round the side of the house and through the broken gate—really, he should fix it—and up on to the sea wall.

He stopped there, but only because of the drop down to the shingle below, and, ramming his hands in his pockets, he stared out over the moonlit sea and wondered how the hell he'd got himself into this mess and how on earth he could get himself out of it…

CHAPTER SIX

WHAT a tortured man.

Molly didn't follow him. She sensed this was something he had to deal with alone, and anyway she was having doubts now herself.

Well, no, not doubts—she had no doubts—but she was scared to death of what losing him would do to her.

Which was ridiculous. You couldn't lose what you didn't have, and he wasn't hers to lose, she knew that. He belonged to his empire on the other side of the world, and she belonged here. That wasn't the issue. If she was brutally honest, the issue was that she was afraid she'd fail him, fail to give him back the confidence she sensed he'd lost with his leg, and so in many ways she was happy he'd walked away so she didn't have to let anyone else down.

She went upstairs to her room, took off the dress—prickly where it chafed the inside of her arms, and heavy, hanging on her shoulders like a dead weight now—and pulled on her soft old jog bottoms and a fleecy top. Then she went downstairs and stood in the sitting room with her arms wrapped round her waist, staring out at him on the sea wall.

Utterly alone.

She couldn't leave him there.

She made tea, scooped up one of the car rugs, which were still by the door, and went out to him. He hadn't moved a muscle, standing there like a sentinel, hands firmly in his pockets, legs apart, shoulders braced for the blow.

Pride in every line of his body.

She didn't speak, just spread the rug out on the edge of the wall and sat down at one end of it, putting the tea in the middle. For a moment she thought he would just ignore her, or walk away, but then he took his hands out of his pockets and joined her, with his legs dangling over the wall and his tea cradled in his hands.

'I'm sorry.'

His voice was rough and she bled for him. 'Don't be,' she said softly. 'I pushed you.'

'No.' He turned his head towards her. 'No, it's not really about you. It's about Celia—my ex.' He paused, swallowed hard, then said expressionlessly, 'She threw up when she saw my leg.'

Molly felt her anger rise at this unknown, stupid woman who'd destroyed his body image and damaged him more than she could ever imagine. 'After the amputation?'

'No—no, before, when it had the fixator on and all the stitches and bandages and drains and stuff. I couldn't blame her, it was pretty gross. I threw up myself when I saw it. She didn't stick around long enough to see it after I lost it.'

'Stupid woman.'

'No. Just superficial and self-serving. It took me a while to work it out. Two years, probably. If I hadn't been trying to get her back, I would have seen sense and had my leg off sooner, and it would have saved me a lot of grief. But that's just being practical, and I guess there was a bit of me that was fighting it, too.'

'Of course there was. It's a huge loss—a real be-reavement. Of course you fought it.'

He stared at her, then gave a gruff little laugh. 'How did you figure that out?'

'I understand grief when I see it. I'm an expert at that.'

He put his tea down and reached out his hand, and she let him take hers. His fingers were hot from his mug, hot and firm and strong and safe, and she threaded hers through them and hung on.

'Tell me about Robert.'

Her grip on his hand tightened a little, and his fingers closed around hers snugly in response, holding her, offering her silent support while she told him the sad little tale.

'He was twenty-three when I met him, and I was twenty-one. I'd just left art college and he was a teacher. I was doing teaching practice at his school as part of my training, and he asked me what on earth I was doing there. I hated teaching, but I wanted a career that would give me time to paint. He pointed out that giving every-thing to pupils left little emotional energy for creativity. He was an art teacher, and he used to paint until he started teaching, then he dried up. He told me to paint, said he'd support me because he had faith in me and knew I could make a success of my art.

'I asked him why he didn't give up and concentrate on painting, and he said he didn't have my talent, and anyway, he was happy teaching, but I owed it to myself to explore my gift. He said not doing that would be to throw it away.'

'Wise man. So what did you do?'

'I moved in with him, dropped my course, started painting big-time and we had Charlie. And then he had a car accident, on his way to an interview for a job I'd made him apply for. He ended up on life-support, and I wouldn't let them turn it off. I said he'd come back to us, I knew he would, so I went and sat with him every night, all night, and in the day I took Charlie in to see him. Then he went into multi-organ failure.'

She trailed off, seeing Robert's face again, the ventilator, the tape on his eyes, the tubes and wires and bleeps and hushed voices all crowding in on her. She dragged in a breath and sat up, staring out at the sea, watching the slow, lazy swell of the waves, hearing instead of the bleeps the soft suck of the water on the shingle, calming and centring her.

'The monitors all went wild and they came running,' she carried on softly. 'They'd wanted to do it days before, but I wouldn't let them. Now, though, I wanted to turn off the machine myself, to let him go. It was my fault he was in there, and my fault he was still suffering, still trapped when he should have been at peace. It needed to be me that let him go. So I turned off the machine, and gave him his peace, but he couldn't give me mine back. It's gone for ever. Like I told you, I can't fix things, so I don't try any more. When I interfere, try to alter the course of things, it all goes wrong. So I paint, and I keep out of the way, and I don't give advice.'

'Is that why you didn't follow me just now? Because you didn't want to interfere with the course of events?'

'Probably. Or it might have been cowardice.'

'I don't think so, Molly. I don't think you're a coward. I think you're sad and confused and blaming yourself for something that wasn't your fault. Were you driving?'

She sighed, knowing where this was going. 'No. No, he was.'

'And did he want to apply for the job?'

She bit her lip. 'Yes, actually it was him that brought it up, but he didn't think he could do it. It was quite a big promotion for him, and he didn't—I just thought I was supporting him, but actually I made him die. So it was right that I was the one to turn off the machine.'

'Molly, it wasn't your fault. All you were doing was giving him the support he gave you over your career choices. You weren't driving, it wasn't your fault he crashed, and you only reacted how anyone else would have reacted under the circumstances.'

'That's not the point. The point is I made it my fault. It was my fault that it dragged on for weeks when it could have been over. He wasn't even there any more. I made him suffer, and he wasn't even there any more, so it was all for nothing.'

'So he didn't suffer—not if he wasn't there.'

She looked at him, hearing the simple, obvious truth that couldn't really change anything, and smiled. 'Don't be logical,' she said gently. 'I'm a woman. I can do guilt for England.'

'Like dippy eggs.'

'And soldiers.'

He smiled at that and held up his arm. 'Come here.'

She moved the mugs and shuffled over to him, slipping easily under his arm, her arms around his waist and her head against his shoulder. It felt so good and right and natural and, as she sat there, she felt peace steal over her, as if, at last, she'd been able to let Robert go, to forgive herself for loving him too much and fighting to save him when she should have said goodbye.

As David had said, all she'd really done was support him in his decision, give him the courage to try for what he wanted, as he'd done with her. She did it all the time with Charlie. What was the difference? Maybe she just hadn't been ready to hear all the well-worn arguments before, but David was the first person she'd talked to about it for ages, and maybe now she was ready to hear it.

And ready to step back into life?

Yes.

She lifted her head and pressed her lips against his chin. 'Take me to bed.'

His jaw tensed beneath her lips, the muscle working. 'It's not pretty,' he warned.

She sat up, pulling herself away. 'Don't confuse me with the shallow, self-serving Celia, please. I would have had Robert back with a plate in his skull and quadriplegia, just because of who he was, who he'd been. For better, for worse and all that. You won't scare me off, David.'

'But we aren't married.'

'So why are you so worried about it? You can walk away.'

'Not easily. Not once I take my leg off.'

'Well, then, we'd better not set fire to the bed.'

He laughed, then got to his feet and tugged her up, scooping up the mugs and the blanket in his free hand and sliding his arm round her shoulders and pulling her close. 'You're a crazy woman, do you know that?' he murmured, and she chuckled and tucked her hand into the back of his trousers and felt the solid warmth of his muscles shifting against her palm as he walked with her back to the cabin.

He put the blanket and the mugs down, then stood in front of her, his eyes meeting hers. 'Are you sure?' he said softly, and she nodded.

'Absolutely,' she told him, although the only thing she was really sure of was that she was going to hurt so much more when he went away, but knowing that she couldn't let him go without doing this, without taking the time they had and giving him something positive to take back with him to his life.

If she could do that, then it would be enough.

She reached up, took the bow-tie that was dangling round his neck and slowly pulled it free. She dropped it on the floor, then reached for his hands and removed his cuff-links, putting them on the bedside table next to the little packet he'd acquired on the way home.

His watch followed them, then she slipped the buttons free one by one, pulled his shirt-tails out of his trousers and slid the shirt off his shoulders, pressing her lips to his chest, feeling the texture of the hair scattered across his skin, the warmth of his body, the beat of his heart beneath her cheek.

The shirt dropped to the floor, and she stepped back and pulled the fleece over her head, dropping it next to his shirt and lifting her eyes to his.

He was motionless, only his eyes moving, tracking slowly over her breasts, taking his time, making her ache for him to touch her. She thought he was never going to, but then he lifted his hand and grazed the back of his knuckles lightly over the shadowed valley between her breasts.

'Do you know, the first time I met you there was a leaf here?' he murmured gruffly. 'And I was jealous of it.'

And, bending his head, he trailed his lips over the path his knuckles had followed, stealing her breath and leaving her trembling for more.

His hands slid down inside the waistband of her jog bottoms, easing them down over her hips so they fell away, and she was left standing in her underwear, grateful for her one little indulgence.

He sucked in his breath, ran his hand over her ribs, down over the flat bowl of her pelvis, turning it so his palm was against her skin as he slid it round behind her and eased her against him. She gasped as they came into contact, the slightly rough texture of his chest tantalising against the sensitive skin of her aching breasts, and she heard his breath catch, too.

'Beautiful,' he said roughly, and then, anchoring her head with his other hand, he lowered his mouth to hers and kissed her properly for the first time.

She opened to him, felt the hot, wet satin of his tongue as it tangled with hers, felt rather than heard his groan as he deepened the kiss, slanting his head to increase the contact and lifting her against him so she could feel his body's surging response. There was too much between them still, the fine wool and silk mix of those beautifully cut trousers just frankly in the way. She reached for the belt, but he eased away, lifted his head and stared down at her, his hands on hers.

'Can we lose the light?' he said, and she realised he was still afraid of her reaction.

'No,' she said, not knowing at all if it was the right thing to say but just sure she wanted to see him, wanted him to see her, so there would be no secrets, nothing left to shock or surprise or disappoint. She lifted her hand and touched it to his heart. 'I want to see you. I want to look into your eyes. I want to know it's you, and I want you to know it's me, warts and all.'

'You have warts?'

His eyes were smiling, and she chuckled. 'No, I don't have warts. I have stretch marks, though. And an appendix scar.'

He stared down at her for an endless moment, then gave a little twisted smile, the smile in his eyes dying. 'Have it your way, then,' he said and, without another word he reached for his belt.

What the hell was she doing?

All the time he was undressing, taking his leg off, going through the whole routine of cleaning and creaming and getting the crutches ready for the night, she just sat there beside him on the bed, looking utterly gorgeous and waiting patiently for him to finish.

He hung on to his boxers, though, just because he didn't want to be stark naked when she threw up on him, and then finally he lifted his head and met her eyes, expecting pity and revulsion, and she smiled. Smiled, for God's sake, as if she was pleased with him. He could imagine her smiling at Charlie like that when he'd done something she was proud of. Or maybe not quite like that—

'It's a bit chilly out here. Can we get under the quilt?'

He raised a brow. 'Are you sure about that? You've finished putting me through hoops?'

'Don't be self-pitying and sarcastic,' she chided and, pushing him to his feet—correction, foot—she pulled the quilt out from under him and slid under it, patting the sheet beside her.

He lay down, his heart going like a train, and then she reached out and cradled his face, lifting herself up so she could stare down into his eyes. 'Kiss me,' she whispered, and he reached up and took her into his arms, his breath leaving him in a rush as he felt the silk of her skin against his, the slight roughness of her lacy bra teasing his chest. It was the one from the washing pile, the most outrageously sexy garment he'd seen in a very long while, and he nearly lost it there and then.

He ran his hand down her back and cupped her bottom, the soft, round globes naked except for that matching sliver of lace that really couldn't be called underwear. He dispensed with the tiny pants, pulled her up against him again and, meshing his mouth with hers, kissed her as if his life depended on it.

Her hands were on him, pushing his boxers out of the way, and he kicked them off, found the clip on her bra and freed the glorious, soft mounds of her breasts that had mesmerised him now for days. He buried his face in them, revelling in the silky texture of her skin. His lips tracked over her, his mouth finding and suckling deeply on nipples tightly pebbled with desire, and her legs clenched around his thigh. She was whimpering, her hands clawing at him, and he dragged her hard up against him and rocked against her with a shuddering groan.

He was going to die if he didn't have her and, reaching for the bedside table, he found the little packet and broke into it with trembling fingers.

'Let me,' she said, and he gritted his teeth and fought for the last shreds of his control.

He was gorgeous.

Simply, utterly gorgeous.

She'd never been loved like that. Oh, Robert had been a good and generous lover, a tender and compassionate man, but this—this was entirely different, elemental, leaving every cell in her body wide awake and screaming with joy. She waited for the twinge of disloyalty, but it didn't come. This wasn't about the past, it was about now, and it was going to be short enough without guilt and recriminations.

He was lying on his back, arms locked behind his head, watching her.

'What is it?'

'You. You're gorgeous.'

He gave a shaky laugh and looked away. 'And you're deluded. Georgie was right, you're far too good for me.'

'Nonsense.' She eased the quilt down, her hands gentle as she ran them over him, massaging the muscles with long, easy strokes. 'Utterly gorgeous. Look at yourself. So strong, so sleek, so clever—beautiful.'

He tipped his head slightly, a puzzled grin teasing at his mouth. 'Clever?'

'Oh, yes,' she said with a slow smile and, bending forwards, she pressed her lips to his chest. 'How's your side?' she asked, and he shifted so she could see it. She frowned. 'Ouch, naughty tree,' she said softly, and feathered her lips over the bruised skin, then slid them down, across his waist, over his hip-bone, down the hair-strewn muscled shaft of his left thigh.

She heard the sharp inward hiss of his breath as he tensed, almost heard the defences clattering into place, but she wasn't going to let him push her away. She turned back the quilt, knelt at his side and let her hands trail over his thigh and down to his knee, her fingertips learning his body, sampling the textures of skin and hair over taut, powerful muscle and solid bone, marvelling at the exquisite perfection of this man.

Then she bent her head and pressed her lips to the neat, hardly visible scar that ran around the front of his shin, where his leg had been so cruelly abbreviated, and she felt him flinch. Her heart aching for him, she curled her hand under the back of his knee and held it tenderly, resting her cheek against his shin.

It was wet, she realised. She touched her tongue to it and tasted salt, and frowned as another drop joined it.

Tears.

Oh, Lord, she could cry a river for this man.

She closed her eyes and laid her cheek against his thigh, taking a moment to steady herself before she lifted her head, but when she did his eyes were closed, and she saw a glistening trail running from the outer corner of his eye down into his temple above the clenched muscle of his jaw.

Oh, David. Oh, my love.

She lay down beside him, kissing away the tears, and with a shuddering sigh he wrapped his arms around her and hung on.

'You're amazing, do you know that?' he said gruffly, after an age. 'Beautiful and kind and generous and so damn sexy—'

His lips pressed to her forehead, and she lifted her head and met his eyes with a smile. 'Are you OK? Only you're talking rubbish now, David. I'm just me.'

'I'm much more than OK, and I'm not talking rubbish. You're beautiful. Come here. I need to make love to you again.'

Her smile widened. 'I thought you'd never ask.'

* * *

'I think I should tell my father.'

Molly turned her head and frowned at him in the early morning light. 'Tell him what? That you've spent the night with me?'

David laughed. 'No. That's none of his business.' His smile faded. 'I meant about my leg.'

She sat up next to him, hauling the quilt up round her shoulders, and he eased himself up the bed beside her and wrapped his arms round her, cocooning her in his warmth. 'I thought you didn't want to tell him before the wedding.'

'I didn't. But then it occurred to me that it might be better for him to know how much I love him and how much I wanted to be there for him when he had his heart attack and his surgery. I let them think I'd broken my ankle, but as an excuse that could only work for so long without arousing suspicion, and after a while they thought I didn't care—particularly Georgie. But I did care, Molly. I so wanted to be at his bedside, and to be at Georgie's wedding, but I couldn't tell them, just because I didn't want to hurt them. But I have, just by protecting them from the truth. And now I think he needs to know, so I can look him in the eye on his wedding day without seeing disappointment. But is that for me, or for him? I just don't know.'

She was silent, simply because she didn't know what to say and didn't feel she could interfere, and after a moment he gently turned her head so he could look at her. 'Well? You're the family relationships expert. What do I do?'

She closed her eyes briefly, unable to bear that gentle, penetrating gaze. 'David, don't ask me to tell you what to do.'

'Well, what would you do if you were me?'

'Tell him,' she said instantly. 'But you know me—speak first, think later. Whereas you probably think too much and keep it all to yourself.'

'Do I?'

'Mmm. I mean, I still don't know.'

He frowned. 'Know what?'

'How you lost your leg.'

'Oh.' He looked away. 'You really want to know? It isn't nice.'

'I didn't imagine it would be,' she told him truthfully, and braced herself for the details she hoped would shed some light on the fallout from the accident.

He sucked in his breath, then let it out in a gusty sigh. 'I was down in Byron. It was late winter—August. There'd been a storm—cold water from the Antarctic meeting the warm tropical water carried down by the East Australian Current. The fish were sheltering close to the shore and the sharks had come in to feed on them. There were lots of little pleasure craft out, and people swimming, and everybody was screaming because of the sharks, but then suddenly the screaming changed and I knew someone had been attacked. I'd spotted the sharks, and I was trying to turn back the kayakers and get them back to shore, and I saw a child in the middle of it, and the water was red. I took the boat in between the child and the shark, dived in and grabbed him and passed him up to the guy who was with me, and then in the panic two of the boats collided and the stern of one swung round and the propeller clipped my ankle just as I was dragging myself up into my boat.'

She felt sick. 'I thought you were going to say the shark got you,' she said unsteadily, but he shook his head.

'No. Nothing so straightforward. It was only a small shark, it probably wouldn't have done as much damage to me as it had done to the boy, but I fell back in and it tried to have a go as well. Anyway, then someone apparently dragged me into a boat and they got me ashore and flew me to Cairns and the rest you know. I don't really remember anything after that till I woke up in hospital.'

'And the child?' she asked softly, knowing the answer, and he shook his head, his throat working.

'He didn't make it. He'd lost too much blood. That's the really galling thing. It was all for nothing.'

She shook her head and cuddled closer to him, sliding her arms round his waist and hugging him tight. 'It wasn't all for nothing, David. If you hadn't tried, if you'd left him, you wouldn't have been able to live with yourself.'

'How do you know that?'

'Don't be ridiculous,' she said, straightening up. 'This is the man who won't tell his father the truth because he doesn't want to worry him! And you truly expect me to believe you'd leave a child to die and never look back? Don't be absurd.'

She felt some of the tension go out of him, and his arm tightened around her shoulders and drew her back against him. 'OK, I'll give you that, but still, there are times when it all seems so bloody pointless.'

'Of course, but at least you can look forward now and move on.'

'Maybe.' He pressed his lips to her hair, and she tilted her head and kissed him back. 'Anyway, enough about that. I want to talk about fantasies.'

She blinked and laughed. 'Fantasies?'

'Yeah.' He grinned and slid down the bed, taking her

with him. 'If we had room service, what would you order for breakfast? Bearing in mind we didn't eat last night and the seagulls would have had our chips.'

'Yes. I'd forgotten that. Oh, boy. Room service fantasies. I don't really like eating in bed, it's too messy. Is that a problem?'

He chuckled, his chest rumbling. 'No. No problem. You can eat wherever you like.'

'Um—well, eggs Benedict, served on the veranda. With Parma ham and smoked salmon, and homemade hollandaise, washed down with tea, and followed by— ooh—pain au chocolat, probably, or a nice juicy apple Danish, with freshly brewed coffee.'

'Black or white?'

'White—with cream. Single cream. Not too much, just enough to be utterly indulgent. And I'd dunk the pastry, I'm afraid. I'm disgusting like that. What about you?'

'A fruit platter—tropical fruits like mango, papaya, pomelo, kiwi—all sorts, whatever's available. Then, yeah, the eggs Benedict sounds nice, and probably an almond croissant. And coffee, black and strong and hot. And I'd dunk, too.'

'Just ring the bell,' she said, with a grin, her laughter abruptly arrested as he threw off the quilt and leapt out of bed.

'David!'

She grabbed him, catching his arm and stopping him just in time, and he fell back again on the edge of the mattress, his face ashen as he stared down at his leg.

For a moment he said nothing, then he turned his head and stared at her, his eyes wide with shock. 'I'd forgotten,' he said hoarsely. 'I'd just completely forgotten.'

She scooted over and slid her arms round him. 'I'm sorry.'

'No. Don't be. Don't be sorry for anything. It's you,' he said, his voice ragged. 'You made me forget, Molly. You made me feel whole again.'

And, cupping her face in his hands, he kissed her tenderly, reverently, then pressed his lips to her hair as he cradled her against his chest. She could feel his heart pounding, but then gradually it slowed and finally he let her go, his eyes still slightly dazed, and, reaching under the bed, he pulled out a pair of crutches.

'I'm going to grab a quick shower and get dressed, then I'm going shopping.'

'Shopping?'

'Uh-huh. For breakfast.'

She sat bolt upright. 'But that's my job! I'm supposed to be your landlady!'

He reached out and brushed his knuckles over her cheek, a tender smile on his lips. 'Not today. Today, just be my lady. Please?'

She felt tears well in her eyes. She'd love nothing more than to be his lady, today and every other day for the rest of her life. She nodded. 'OK. Just today. Can I get up and shower while you're gone or do I have to stay here?'

'You can do whatever you like. I won't be long. And then I'm going to cook you your fantasy room-service breakfast.'

CHAPTER SEVEN

HE WASN'T long.

Molly only had time to shower and dry her hair, and she was just putting on a clean pair of jeans when she heard the car pull up outside. She watched him coming back in, shopping bags in one hand, whistling under his breath as he walked up the garden, and he looked up and saw her at her bedroom window and blew her a kiss, and she hurriedly threw on a top and ran downstairs to him.

'Can I help?'

'No. Go and sit down outside in the sun. It's lovely. I'll bring you breakfast in a minute.'

'Star,' she said and, going up on tiptoe, she kissed his cheek, still rough with stubble and infinitely exciting, and, resisting the urge to drag him back to bed, she went out on to the veranda and found a single red rose lying on the table.

Tears welled in her eyes, and she sat and held it and wondered what on earth she'd done to deserve this brief and precious moment in time with him.

She took back everything she'd thought about him and relationships. He was the most amazing, wonderful, complex, thoughtful man she'd ever met, and she couldn't even begin to contemplate what her life would be like when he'd gone.

'Breakfast, milady.'

He was balancing a tray groaning with goodies on one hand and, as she watched, he unloaded it item by item, setting each one down with quiet precision.

A fruit platter, a pot of tea and fresh cups, a little jug of milk, another of cream, a coffee press, a steaming basket of pastries—it went on and on.

'Good grief,' she said, watching in awe. 'Real coffee—and napkins?'

'Only paper. They didn't have linen.'

He gave a few deft flicks of the wrist and folded it into an intricate shape like a swan.

'How on earth did you do that?'

'Years of practice,' he said with a chuckle, and put the swan down in front of her. 'Try the fruit. It's gorgeous.'

It was, and she was doing well until she speared a slice of mango and the juice dribbled down her chin.

'Oops,' he said and, leaning over, he captured the juice with his tongue, following the trail up to her lips and kissing them.

'I'll have to do that again,' she said with a smile, and he chuckled.

'Feel free.'

He disappeared into the kitchen again when they'd finished the fruit, and reappeared a couple of minutes later with two plates. 'Eggs Benedict, as ordered,' he said, and set them down with a flourish. Perfectly poached eggs, each cradled on a nest of smoked salmon and Parma ham supported by a round—literally—of toast and topped by fresh, warm hollandaise sauce which he must have whipped up while she'd been waiting. She'd heard him beating something, but she couldn't believe he'd actually made it fresh. And it was perfect. Delicious. Mouthwatering and delicate and probably the best thing she'd ever tasted in her life.

She said so and, to her surprise, he coloured slightly. 'Thank you,' he said, as if it really mattered what she thought, and, leaning over, he kissed her.

'Am I dribbling again?' she said with a laugh.

He shook his head. 'Not this time. That was just because I wanted to kiss you. Now eat up, the pastries are getting cold.'

'So,' she said, after she'd torn a chocolate croissant in half and dipped it in her coffee and sucked the soggy mess in ecstasy, 'how come you can cook so well?'

He gave a wry smile. 'My father's fault. He hoped I'd follow him into the business, and he insisted that I learn everything from the ground up, so there wasn't a job I couldn't do or a process I didn't understand. He said you can't know if people are doing a good job or being unreasonable about something if you don't understand what it is you're asking them to do. And he's right. So I've applied it to everything I do. I've been involved in the building or renovation of every hotel we've got, I can do the maintenance, balance the books, make the beds, clean the bathrooms, cook the food, wait tables, make cocktails—I've even been known to play the piano in the bar when the entertainment didn't show. And I'm the dive master and I take the dive boats out, I've built the canopy walk at the retreat and I can do the guided tour, although we have someone with far more experience to do it on a regular basis.'

She realised she was staring at him open-mouthed, and she shut her mouth and turned her attention back to her pastry. 'Um—that's pretty multi-talented.'

He chuckled. 'You know the saying "Jack of all trades but master of none"? Well, that's pretty much me, but I certainly understand the principles and I can step in and take over in an emergency without letting the side down. But I can't make soufflés, for some reason. They just hate me.'

She let out her breath on a little laugh and smiled at him. 'Well, thank God for small mercies. Something you can't do!'

'I can't paint, either. Well, as in art. Robert was right to support you. You've got an astonishing gift. I can't tell you how I envy you that.'

She cocked her head on one side. 'But your hotels are successful?'

'Oh, yes. They're doing well. We're really pleased.'

'So you can do things well.'

He smiled. 'I get by,' he admitted, wondering what she'd say if she could see the paper value of his empire. Probably something pretty damning, but it hadn't been deliberate. It was all down to luck and chance and hard work.

Lots of hard work. His father would understand that. Maybe even approve. If only he could talk to him openly.

'I'm going to see my father later. What time do you have to pick up Charlie?'

'Oh—Georgie's going to phone. I think she's keeping him most of the day.'

'In which case, shall we move the stuff up to your new room, and then you can get settled in before tonight?'

'Really? What about the washing-up?'

He laughed. 'Why don't we leave it for the scullery maid?'

'That'll be me, then,' she said with a smile, and stood up. 'I'll do it later. Come on, let's go.'

It looked really good.

It had been a bit of a struggle getting the mattress up the stairs, but now everything was in, the bed was made— and christened—and they were lying in it side by side staring out over the sea and admiring their handiwork.

Beside him, Molly gave a contented sigh and smiled up at him. 'Thank you,' she said softly. 'I couldn't have done it without you, and now tomorrow I can get all my art stuff moved and start work on that exhibition.'

'I've been meaning to talk to you about that,' he began, but then the phone rang, and with a wordless little grumble she got out of bed and ran downstairs to answer it, grabbing his shirt en route. He heard her say his sister's name and, throwing back the covers, he dressed quickly.

She appeared in the doorway as he finished, hesitating on the threshold. That transparent face was troubled, and he straightened up.

'What is it?'

'That was Georgie.'

'I heard. I take it you have to go and get Charlie.'

She nodded. 'We're invited for an early supper— and she said I've got to bring you. She wants a word,' she added with wry emphasis.

He sighed. 'Why am I always in trouble with my sister? You'd think she was older than me. She's such a headmistress.'

'I think she feels we should have stayed longer last night.'

'Oh, stuff that. I did my bit,' he said, turning away and looking for his shirt, then remembering she was wearing it and giving up. 'Oh, well, I suppose we should go. She'll only get worse if we don't.'

'Maybe you should tell her.'

He snorted, and took the shirt she was now holding out to him. Which left her naked, and he looked at her, at the lovely peaches-and-cream perfection of her skin, the soft rose of her nipples pebbling in the cool air, and rammed his arms into the sleeves.

'Get dressed,' he said gruffly, 'or there's no way we'll get there.'

He pulled her into his arms, kissed her gently and let her go. 'I'll make some coffee,' he said and, leaving her to it, he went downstairs and wondered if anybody would notice if he strangled his sister.

Unfair. She was only protecting her beloved father, the father she thought he was neglecting and rejecting.

Time to tell them.

But how?

He hadn't got the slightest clue.

Georgie was waiting for them when they arrived.

His father's car was there, and Nick's, and Georgie's, but no others, he was relieved to see. The others had obviously collected their children earlier, and so it was just family.

And Molly, of course, who, as a close friend of Liz and her matron of honour at the wedding next week, was practically family as well.

As they got out of the car they could hear the children playing in the garden. The boys had a tree-house in the little bit of woodland just behind the house, and David could hear whoops and yells and Tarzan noises coming from that direction.

Boys being boys, he thought, and felt a pang of envy. It seemed like for ever since he'd had that much energy and enthusiasm.

They came charging round the corner of the house and skidded to a halt. 'Can Charlie stay?' Dickon begged, jumping up and down, and Molly reached out and hugged him briefly.

'Only till after supper. Your mother's had enough of you all racing around, I'm sure.'

'She's been playing with the girls,' Charlie said. 'Nick's been outside with us. We were playing football.'

Oh, hell, he thought, but then looked up and there was Georgie, her face unsmiling, and if it hadn't been for Molly he would have turned on his heel and walked away.

'Can we have a word?' she said stiffly, and he knew it was time.

Time to stop pretending that everything was all right and he was just an arrogant bastard who didn't care about his family, time to get it all out into the open and have done with it.

'Good idea,' he said and, ignoring the rest of them, he followed her back into the house and through to a little sitting room overlooking the sea. 'Fire away, then,' he said, standing by the window and staring at the lazy swell, wishing he was out on it, sitting in a little boat with a line in the water and nothing to worry about except catching his next meal.

'Sit down,' she said, and he raised a brow, but he sat anyway, if only because she was pregnant and he didn't want her stressed any more than she would be when she found out.

'Why did you go so early last night? You know how important it was to Dad to have you there.'

'Because I was sick of being lectured on my short-comings by the entire population of Yoxburgh,' he said truthfully.

She frowned. 'Who was doing that?'

'Everyone—starting with you, mainly.'

'I didn't say a word last night.'

'Except to tell Molly she was too good for me and you were going to find her someone who deserved her.'

Her jaw dropped, and she shook her head. 'David, that was a joke.'

'Really? Sorry, I must have missed the punch-line.'

She coloured and closed her eyes. 'I'm sorry. It's just—I'm very fond of Molly, and I know you'll hurt her.'

'Let's leave Molly out of this.'

'You brought her name up, and you can't deny it. You've always been a heartbreaker, David. You've never thought about anyone but yourself.'

'That isn't true.'

'Isn't it? In which case, why didn't you come home for my wedding? Why didn't you come back for Dad's heart surgery? You had a broken ankle, for God's sake! That's not a reason, it's an excuse!'

He looked down, knowing he had to do this now, and trying to find words that wouldn't hurt her. Or him.

'It was rather more than that.'

'How? I mean, clearly it's sorted—you don't even have a limp, so it can't have been that bad! Liz had a really nasty injury and she's still limping, but she was up and about again a damn sight quicker than three years! So we all know it's nothing to do with your ankle. Dad thinks there's something wrong—that your busi-ness is in trouble, or you're gay or something, or you've got cancer or HIV—'

'He thinks that?' he said, stunned.

'Amongst other things. Well, what did you expect, David? You've been avoiding us like the plague—you won't answer your phone, you don't ring—you've been better the last few months, but only because we've had the wedding to talk about and plan, but without it I doubt if we would have heard a squeak out of you. You hole up on the other side of the world, out of touch—I mean, what were we supposed to think? Get real!'

'Real? You want real?' he said, his voice hollow to his ears, and he made an effort to soften it. 'You want to know why I don't limp? Because it doesn't hurt any more, Georgie, because I no longer have it. My leg was amputated last summer.'

She stared at him, trying to make sense of his words, then she sucked in her breath, stared at his feet and covered her mouth with her hands.

'No-o-o!' she wailed and, jumping to her feet, she ran for the door, just as Nick came in.

'Georgie? Darling, what on earth—? What the hell have you said to my wife?' he demanded, turning on David with rage in his eyes.

'I told her the truth—at last. And I need to talk to her—'

'Leave her alone!'

Nick blocked his way, but a brick wall wouldn't have stopped him at that point. Grabbing his shoulder, he thrust him out of the way and pushed past, following the sound of sobbing along the hall and up a narrow little staircase. The tower? He came out at the top into a room overlooking the sea, and found Georgie slumped in a heap on the sofa, great rending sobs tearing her apart.

'Georgie?'

He knelt awkwardly beside her, pulling her into his arms, and she burrowed into his chest, the sobbing escalating until he thought she'd damage herself.

'Georgie, sweetheart, stop it, it's OK.'

'It's not OK,' she sobbed. 'I've been so cruel to you—why didn't you tell me? Why did you shut me out? I'm your sister, I should have been there for you—'

'How? You were here with Dad, doing what I couldn't do, supporting him, saving his business, taking the workload off him—you couldn't have been with me, and nor could Dad. I had no choice but to shut you out.'

She pushed herself upright and looked at him, her eyes filling again. 'You went through all that alone,' she said tearfully, biting her lip, and he shifted so he was sitting beside her and drew her gently back into his arms.

'I was OK. I was off my head on morphine for the first few weeks, and then I realised I was getting addicted so I stopped taking it. Stopped taking everything. Which made the next two years pretty dire, but then I met someone who'd had an amputation, and I realised it was the only way forward. They couldn't do anything for me that would make it right, and I'd always known that in my heart. So I had it amputated—on the day you phoned to tell me Dad was getting married again. You know I told you I was going into a meeting and I'd be out of touch for a few days? The nurse was in the room waiting to take me to theatre.'

'No.' She lifted a hand and cupped his cheek gently, her face soaked with tears. 'Oh, David, no. I didn't have a clue.'

'That was rather the idea,' he said wryly, and she punched him gently in the chest and then snuggled back against him.

'When are you going to tell Dad?'

'After the wedding.'

'I think you should tell him before. He's really worried. His imagination's been running riot.'

'Damn.' He sighed. 'I didn't want to upset him—'

'David, he's already upset. We all are. It's the only way to put it right. And it will put it right, because look at you. I didn't have the slightest idea, so obviously it's not restricting your life drastically—unless you were lying about taking a group of guests diving the other week when we spoke?'

'No. No, I wasn't lying. I can dive. I can do most things.'

Including making love, apparently, he thought, but that wasn't for Georgie's consumption.

'So tell him. I'll help you, if you like. I know it must be really hard.'

He hugged her. 'Actually, it's a relief. It's been killing me for years. I hate lying to you all. I think you need to tell Nick, though. He was ready to kill me.'

'Nick won't kill you.'

David wasn't so sure, but then he lifted his head and looked towards the stairs, and met Nick's sombre eyes through the banisters. He must have followed him up. Of course. He would have done the same.

'May I join you?' he asked quietly, and David nodded.

'Of course. I'm sorry.'

'Don't be. Georgie, are you all right, darling?'

He crouched down in front of her and took her hands in his and, as David watched, her eyes filled with tears again and she nodded. 'I'm fine. I feel such a bitch.'

David patted her shoulder and stood up. 'Don't beat yourself up, kid. It isn't your fault, it's mine. You stay here with Nick for a bit, get yourself together. I'm going to see Dad.'

'No! I'll come. I'm all right, David. It was just the shock, but I think I should be there with you. I want to be.' And, getting to her feet, she hugged him hard, and led the way back downstairs.

'Are you OK?'

He smiled a little crookedly.

'I'm fine,' he said softly, coming up the steps to the veranda where she'd been waiting for him, and now he was in the light she could see that his eyes were red-rimmed, but the strain was gone from the corners, and his smile, although crooked, was relieved. 'A bit wrung-out, but OK. How did you get home?'

'Liz gave us a lift. She said you all needed to talk, and Nick was putting the children to bed. Was it OK?'

He nodded. 'He knew something was going on, he just didn't know what. If I'd realised that, I would have told him ages ago and put him out of his misery. He's been waiting for three years for me to confide in him, and there were a lot of tears, but I feel so much better and I'm really glad I've done it.'

'Good. I thought you would be. Have you eaten?'

'Not much. It was all a bit fraught for food and Georgie was exhausted. I wouldn't mind a sandwich and some coffee, but I can make it.'

'Let me,' she said and, leaving him on the veranda, she went into the kitchen and put the last of the smoked salmon left over from breakfast into thick slices of the wholemeal bread he'd bought that morning. There was nothing elegant about it, but he didn't need elegance, she thought, he needed comfort, and that was exactly what she intended to give him.

She made a pot of tea—not coffee, because she didn't

want to keep him awake—and piled it all on to a tray and took it out to him. It was cold out there, but somehow she knew he needed to be out in the open tonight, and she had already been wearing her coat to sit and wait for him.

'Here,' she said, putting the tray down.

'Aren't you having any?'

'I ate with the children,' she told him. 'It was all ready when you disappeared with your father and Nick and Georgie, and I took Liz on one side and told her. I hope you don't mind. I could see from Georgie's face that you'd told her.'

'Yeah. Not very subtly, unfortunately, but it's a bit hard to be subtle about something like that. Thanks for telling Liz. She needed to know, so she could be there for my father. So, what's in this doorstop?'

She laughed. 'Smoked salmon and a squeeze of lemon juice.'

'Fabulous,' he said and, picking it up, he sank his teeth into it and groaned. 'Oh, great,' he mumbled, and she sat back and watched him with a smile on her face that wouldn't go away. He drank two big mugs of tea, disappeared into the kitchen and came back with some of the leftover pastries and shared them with her, feeding her little bites of soft, gooey apple Danish and strips of cinnamon whirl.

And then, when he'd finally come to a halt, he took the wreckage of the tray out to the kitchen, came back and held out his hand to her.

'Come to bed with me,' he said softly, and she couldn't have denied him if she'd wanted to.

They went down to the cabin, and he undressed her slowly, kissing every inch of her as it was revealed, and then thoroughly, meticulously, he kissed her all again, his mouth hot and hard and hungry, until she thought she would scream.

And then he moved over her, and she did scream, but he caught her cries in his mouth and they mingled with his own, and as they died away he rolled to his side and took her with him, wrapping her in his arms and cradling her against his chest until her heart slowed and her breathing returned to normal.

And then he did it all over again.

CHAPTER EIGHT

'MOLLY, it's Liz.'

'Oh, hi, Liz,' Molly said, tucking the phone under her chin and wiping paint off her fingers on to a rag. 'Thanks for the lift last night. How are you all?'

'Actually, we're fine. George is very shocked and saddened, but he's hugely relieved it's none of the other things he'd been afraid of, and he says he can deal with it now he knows, it was the not knowing that was so hard. How's David?'

'Still asleep,' she said, remembering him as she'd left him, sprawled out on the bed as the first fingers of dawn had reached out across the sky and brushed him with gold. She hadn't wanted to leave him, but he was so heavily asleep she thought he'd be there for hours and she didn't want to be out there still when Charlie woke. 'I think he's exhausted.'

'I'm sure. He's really been through it, and George is gutted that he wasn't there for him, but he understands, I think. Can you ask him to call when he's up? We need to talk to you both about the wedding. We were going to do it last night, but events got a little hijacked. It's just a few last-minute details, and George thought maybe you could both come for lunch and bring Charlie, too, if he's not busy.'

'That would be lovely,' she said. 'I'll get David to ring you when he emerges.'

She looked out of the back bedroom window, but the curtains in the cabin were still closed. She could take him tea, she thought, but that was probably just being selfish. And then she saw the curtain move, and with a light-hearted smile she couldn't suppress, she ran downstairs and tapped on the cabin door.

'Well, hi,' he said, drawing her in and closing the door behind her, his smile matching her own. 'Where's Charlie?'

'Crabbing with Bob.'

'Good. That means I can say good morning properly,' he said and, tunnelling his fingers through her hair, he eased her closer, lowered his mouth to hers and brushed it softly, lightly with his lips. 'Good morning,' he murmured, and then kissed her again, little sips and nibbles that made her legs go weak and her blood turn to fire in her veins.

Then he lifted his head and smiled down at her. 'I missed you when I woke up,' he said gruffly.

'Me, too,' she murmured, and she cradled his jaw in her palm, loving the feel of stubble against her skin. He was dressed, but he hadn't shaved yet, and there was something intensely erotic about the sensation that drove common sense out of her head.

She lowered her hand before she forgot what she was meant to be doing, and eased away from his big, hard body. 'Liz rang about the wedding. She wants you to call her when you're up.'

'I'm up,' he said with a lazy, sexy smile, and she

slapped his hands where they had settled, warm and possessive, over her breasts.

'You know what I mean,' she said, laughing. 'They want to talk about some last-minute details. They've invited us all for lunch.'

'All?'

'The three of us.'

'Did you say yes?'

'I did—provisionally. Is that OK?'

He nodded. 'It's fine. Actually, I'm really looking forward to spending time with them. And I've been thinking—we ought to tell Charlie about my leg. Georgie's kids are bound to know, so he has to, really, if you don't have a problem with it.'

She felt a flutter of nerves. 'I don't, and I don't think he will, but I'm not sure about you. He'll be insanely curious, you do know that, don't you?'

He laughed. 'Of course he will. He's an eight-year-old boy. He'll want to know how it all works, but that's cool. I can show him all my different legs and tell him how they work.'

'You have different ones?'

He smiled gently. 'I have three. You can be insanely curious too. I'll let you.'

Charlie was fascinated.

He wanted to try them on, but that, of course, was impossible. He could, however, play with the crutches and he scooted up and down the garden while Molly tried not to hover, then came back to the cabin door and put his head on one side and said, 'Is that why you don't play football?'

David's smile was wry. 'Pretty much. I haven't actually tried, but I'll probably fall over.'

'You could try—carefully,' Charlie suggested tentatively, and Molly could see he was absolutely desperate for his hero to have a go.

David sighed and grinned and got to his feet. 'OK. But I might miss a few balls.'

'That's cool. I miss lots!'

And she watched them kick the ball around the garden for a few minutes, until the inevitable happened and he tripped and fell on to the grass. But he came up laughing, and got to his feet again and kicked the ball back to Charlie, and then after another couple of minutes he looked at his watch. 'We ought to go for lunch.'

'Can we take the football?' Charlie asked eagerly, and David grinned and rumpled his hair.

'Yes, sure. I don't know if I'll have time to play with you, but I'm sure Dad won't mind if you kick the ball around. I did it for years. I nearly wore a hole in the back wall of the garage.'

So they went, in his mother's car, and when George answered the door he welcomed them all in and gathered his son into his arms, his eyes over-bright, while Molly stood and watched and tried to swallow the lump in her throat. 'Come on in,' he said, releasing David at last, and they went through to the kitchen and found Liz busy with a mixing bowl.

She waggled floury fingers at them in greeting. 'I'm making apple crumble for pudding,' she said, and Charlie bounced over to her and asked if he could help.

'Sure. Wash your hands first.'

He went over to the sink, but he couldn't quite reach the tap so David turned it on for him. 'OK?'

'Yup. That's enough.'

And, scrubbing his hands dry on his T-shirt, he ran

back to Liz. 'Did you know David's got three legs?' he said matter-of-factly as he plunged his hands into the bowl and started rubbing in the butter.

'Three?' Liz said in surprise, turning to David, and he gave a wry grin.

'Well, actually, I've got four, if you count the right one,' he corrected with a chuckle, and his father's face contorted for a second, the big, gruff man reduced almost to tears by his son's gentle humour.

'Hey,' David said softly and, putting his arm round his father's shoulders, he gave them a quick squeeze. 'What does a body have to do to get a drink round here?' he added, breaking the tension, and, clearing his throat, George headed for the fridge.

'Tea, coffee, juice, beer, wine, gin and tonic—?'

'Molly?' David prompted.

'Oh, G and T, please! I haven't had one for ages. Just weak, though.'

'Yes, don't get her tiddly, we can't have us both falling over.'

'Falling over?' Liz asked David, and Charlie laughed.

'We played football, but he tripped. He fell over the other day when he was chasing me, too, and the tree hurt him.'

'Not much,' David put in quickly, seeing his father's face. He added, 'It's an occupational hazard. I fall over all the time—only because I do stupid things. It's getting better—maybe I'm slowing down a bit, but when I first got up on my feet again it was such a relief I just got on with it, and it takes a bit of getting used to.'

'I'm sure,' George said, his face awash with emotion, and Molly felt so sorry for him that they hadn't been together at the time and he hadn't been able to share the highs and lows of his son's recovery. If it had been Charlie…

She couldn't even bear to think about that. He was deeply engrossed in the crumble now, his little fingers squashing away at it while Liz supervised and intervened from time to time.

'So—why three legs?' George asked, handing David a can of beer.

'One for the beach so it can get wet and sandy and stuff,' Charlie said, ticking them off on his floury fingers, 'and one for proper swimming—that one's really cool, it's got a sort of pole in the middle and the foot's got a hinge so it can point down so he can wear flippers for diving. Mum, I want to go diving, it sounds really cool.'

'You have to be older,' she said quickly, and caught David's smothered smile.

'And his everyday leg,' Charlie finished triumphantly, ticking off the third finger. 'Oh, and his proper one. Is it ready yet, or do I need to do more?'

'No, I think it's fine,' Liz said, rescuing the crumble before it turned to shortbread. 'Right, we need to bake it first,' she said, helping him to tip it out on to a baking sheet, and then she put it in the oven.

'You've refitted the kitchen,' David said, watching her, and Molly wondered if he resented Liz's influence.

His father smiled ruefully. 'Well, it needed it. It hadn't been done since we bought the house before you were born, and you're—what now? Thirty-two?'

He nodded. 'Thirty-three in October.'

'Well, then. Time enough, I think. And Liz needed a raised oven because of her leg.'

'Oh, don't get me wrong, it looks great, and it was high time. I'm just surprised you didn't move to somewhere more sensible,' he said, but his father just smiled again.

'Why?' he asked. 'It's a happy house, and we have a lot of grandchildren. Maybe more, one day. It's nice to be able to have everybody here.'

And Molly had a sudden yearning to add to those numbers, to be the woman who bore David's children, so that George and Liz could extend their extended family and Charlie could have brothers and sisters and she and David—

She stopped herself right there. There was no future for them, certainly not the sort of future she was busy dreaming up, and she needed to remember that.

And wean Charlie off his hero before his heart, too, was broken irretrievably by the inevitable parting.

It was a lovely day.

They sorted out the wedding details while Charlie kicked the ball around in the garden, then went home—odd, how he thought of leaving his father's house to go to Molly's as going home—only to be joined by Georgie and Nick and their children. They had his father's dog Archie in tow, as well. He seemed to have moved in with them, and he raced around the garden after a Frisbee and kept all the children occupied.

Which was just as well, because Georgie was exhausted.

'You should have stayed at home and rested,' David told her guiltily, but she said that being with her brother was more important to her than resting, and so Molly made him bring out a comfy chair on to the veranda for her, and she sat with her hand in his and they rebuilt bridges while Molly and Nick watched the children and refereed the inevitable squabbles.

Georgie wanted to hear all the gory details again, and in more detail than the slightly edited version he'd given his father—how it had happened, how he'd felt, when each operation had taken place, how he'd got back on his feet—all of it, and so he told her, going through it once more, and oddly, this time, letting it go as he did so, because at last, it seemed, he could move on.

After a while Molly settled the children down with juice and biscuits and brought out some more tea for the adults, and the conversation became more general. They ended up staying for supper, and by the time they left Charlie was more than ready for bed.

Molly took him up, and David cleared up the kitchen and then paced around, restless for some reason. 'Do you mind if I go fishing?' he asked her when she came down again.

She looked at him in surprise. 'Of course I don't mind. You're free to do whatever you want, you don't have to ask me.'

Somehow that wasn't the answer he'd hoped for, but he kissed her cheek and said he'd see her later, and went back out to the cabin to change and find a thick coat. He put on his beach leg, because he was bound to get wet in the boat, and then walked down to the harbour to find Bob.

He was just getting his rods ready, and he looked up and grunted.

'Wondered when you'd turn up.'

'Sorry, I've been busy.'

'Don't have to explain to me, boy. Coming out?'

'Mind the company?'

'Never minded your company, Davey. You can bait my hooks.'

He laughed and picked up Bob's gear. 'Nothing new there, then. I hope you haven't got black lugs.'

'I have.'

'Damn. They stink—and they stain your fingers.'

'Big girl's blouse. Come on, we'll miss the tide.'

He grinned and followed Bob down to the boat, tossing the gear in and climbing carefully aboard. They puttered out of the river mouth, between the buoys that marked the ever-shifting shingle banks, and he dropped anchor just off the shore.

David scanned the shoreline in the deepening gloom, just about making out Georgie's house in the distance, and then to the right, up on the cliff, he noticed a house that he'd never seen before. It stood out, a large rectangular white block with vast areas of glass, almost ghostly in the twilight.

'What's that?' he asked, pointing to it, and Bob looked up from his line and grunted.

'That's Dan Hamilton's house. He built it two years ago. Lovely place—proper posh job. I'm surprised you haven't been.'

He wasn't. He'd been pretty unforthcoming with his old friends, so it wasn't a surprise to him that he hadn't been invited there, or to Harry and Emily's house, and he felt a twinge of regret.

'I've been busy,' he said yet again using it as an excuse, and yet again Bob grunted.

'What about this leg, then?' he said once the lines were baited and in.

'What about it?' David asked, teasing at his line and wondering what he knew.

He certainly hadn't told him much, but the tom-toms might have been working, and Bob was pretty acute.

'Well, I know you lost it,' the old man said bluntly. 'The shoe's a bit of a giveaway. Not as creased. And I know enough people who've lost a leg to know what to look for. And propellers tend to win in an argument. So what did your father make of it? I take it you've told him now?'

'Oh, he was upset, but he'll get over it. I have.'

Another grunt, followed by, 'Can't imagine you letting it hold you back. So—when are you coming home?'

He sighed. 'I'm not. England isn't home any more, Bob. I've got a whole new life out in Australia.'

'Is that right?'

'Yes, it is.'

'Well, I hope it makes you happy,' he said gruffly, and then David's line jerked. 'Ho, you've got a big one on there, boy!' he said. 'Reel 'im in.'

And that was it, subject over, to David's relief, and for the next three hours they hardly spoke at all. Then, as they made their way back in to the jetty with only the soft puttering of the engine to break the quiet of the night, Bob said gruffly, 'Be good to Molly. Don't lead her on. She doesn't deserve any more heartache, son. Nor does the boy.'

'No,' he agreed and, sticking his fingers into the gills, he carried the fish home to Molly, gutted them in the sink and put them in the fridge, wondering if he really was leading her on or if they both knew the score, and even knowing that, whose heart was going to ache the most when he went away.

She came down as he was cleaning up, and sniffed. 'Smells promising,' she said with a smile, and he jerked his head at the fridge.

'Ooh, mackerel for breakfast—and sea bass! Fantastic, we can have that for supper,' she said, peering in, then turned back to him, lifting the kettle in enquiry.

'Tea would be good. I'm awash with Bob's awful coffee from his flask.' He wiped the sink down and hung the cloth over the tap. 'Why are you still up? I would have thought you'd have gone to bed.'

'I've been painting.'

'All this time?'

She smiled softly. 'And waiting up for you. You said you'd see me later.'

He felt himself relax his guard, and realised he'd been tense ever since she'd sent him on his way earlier. Stupid. He'd thought she didn't care, and she was just letting him get on with his life and getting on with hers. It wasn't that she didn't want him. One look into her eyes was enough to tell him that.

He shoved his hands back under the tap and scrubbed them harder to get rid of the yellow stain from the bait…

The days leading up to the wedding were idyllic.

He spent a lot of time with his father, and while he was there Molly painted, getting ready for her exhibition. And when he wasn't there, they painted the cabin.

Well, mostly. Sometimes they took a long, lazy lunch break and went up to the attic and made love, but most of the time they worked together on the house in one way or another, and it really began to show.

He fixed the gate, mended the downpipe and tied the rose back up, then scraped the cabin back to the bare wood and replaced some of the boards using the dangerous-looking gadget with a whirling blade he'd brought back from his father's. A table saw, apparently, and she was glad he put it right away out of Charlie's reach in the cabin every time he'd finished with it for the day, because the thing gave her the creeps.

She loved watching him work—well, apart from when he was using the table saw—and, because the weather was being so kind to them, most of the time he had his shirt off, so she was treated to a glorious view of his body, rippling with muscle under the smooth, tanned skin. And every now and again he'd turn and catch her looking and grin that cheeky, sexy grin which melted her bones.

She wanted to paint him—to capture the essence of him, the elemental power of his body hard at work. But that would have meant capturing an image of him that would linger after he'd gone, and maybe it would be better to let him go.

Except she was fooling herself, of course. He was never going to leave her. He'd always be in her heart, and the images of him would be with her for ever.

So she didn't paint him, she painted canvases for her exhibition, and she painted the cabin with him, and she stored the images in her mental filing system so she could pull them out and look at them when he'd gone away.

Then finally the day of the wedding dawned, and she dropped Charlie off with Robert's parents and headed over to Liz's little flat at Nick's house to help her get ready.

She was, as Molly had expected, utterly calm and relaxed.

'I can't wait,' she said with a smile. 'I've known since I met him that he was special, and three years is more than long enough. And at our age, frankly, it's ridiculous, but we both felt we wanted to be sure. The kids had been through enough. Their only grandparents rushing into and out of a hasty marriage wouldn't have been exactly helpful!'

Molly laughed. 'No, I can see that,' she agreed, but Liz's opening comment about knowing since she'd met him that George was special rang a chord. She'd known that David wasn't just another paying guest who was going to pass through her life and leave it unmarked from the moment she'd turned the corner of her house and come face to face with him in the garden, and the following two weeks had done nothing to change her mind.

What she didn't know, and couldn't begin to work out, was where they went from here.

The wedding was wonderful.

They were married in the parish church, in a short, simple ceremony which David found immensely moving.

So, apparently, did Molly, he discovered when he turned to escort her into the vestry to sign the register as witnesses. Her eyes were over-bright and, as their eyes locked, he found himself wishing for something he couldn't quite begin to get to grips with.

Marriage? To Molly?

Ridiculous.

Or was it?

The reception was held at the newly reopened hotel, in the function room designed for such events. If Georgie hadn't been pregnant, they would have held it at their house, but with four children and another so close it wasn't sensible—and anyway, Molly thought, George had done such a lovely job on the hotel that it was fitting it should host such a celebration.

And they did celebrate. She'd never seen Liz look so happy or relaxed, and George was in fine form.

So, she was rather stunned to see, was David. For the first time he was behaving in public as he did with her, laughing, teasing, flirting with the women and bantering with the men—she could quite see how he'd got his heartbreaker reputation.

And why he made such a successful hotelier.

His speech was short, funny and immensely touching, and once the formal part of the reception was out of the way, he relaxed into the occasion with a vengeance.

Until the dancing started, and then he seemed to withdraw again.

Would she let him?

No. He should dance with her—it was, after all, his job to escort the chief bridesmaid, and apart from all the tiny little flower girls who'd long been tucked up in bed, she was it. And she just knew it was another milestone that he had to overcome.

So she waited, refusing invitations from Harry and Daniel and Nick, and when the music slowed, she stood up and held out her hand to him.

'Dance with me,' she said softly.

He grimaced slightly. 'Molly, I can't—'

'Yes, you can,' she murmured and, after what seemed like an age, he got to his feet and took her hand.

'This is another first, so don't say you weren't warned,' he muttered and, leading her to the dance floor, he took her in his arms. They didn't move much. They didn't need to, it was enough just to hold him and sway to the music, and after a few moments she felt him relax and ease her closer.

'See? I told you you could do it,' she murmured in his ear, and he gave a rusty chuckle.

'I don't call this dancing,' he replied.

'Well, we can jive if you want, but I'll probably fall flat on my face,' she said, and he laughed again, his breath huffing softly against her ear.

'This'll do,' he said and, lowering his head, he kissed her fleetingly and then rested his forehead against hers as they swayed to the slow, intoxicating beat. 'Have I told you how gorgeous you look in that dress?' he murmured, and she shook her head.

'Remiss of me. You look fabulous.' He slid his arms down her back, linking his hands in the hollow of her back and easing her closer. 'Very elegant. Very beautiful. Very, very sexy,' he added, his voice deepening. 'I keep wondering what you're wearing under it. It's driving me crazy. I want to take you to bed right now and peel it off you and find out,' he said softly, and she eased away a little and laughed up at him, her cheeks warming.

'Behave,' she mouthed, and he chuckled and pulled her back again.

'Not a chance. Just don't leave me here or I'll be very embarrassed.'

'I won't, but you need to cool off, because I think your stepmother wants to dance with you.'

'No way. Give me five minutes.'

'We could go outside into the courtyard and cool off.'

'Or I could kiss you.'

'Or both.'

'In the reverse order.'

They left the dance floor and headed outside, and as soon as they were out of sight of the other guests he turned her into his arms and brought his mouth down on hers and kissed her.

Thoroughly.

Her knees buckled, and he caught her up against him with a groan. 'I want you, Molly,' he breathed, and she felt the urgency of his body as he cradled her close. 'You drive me crazy. I need you now.'

'Not here,' she murmured, easing away from him again, and then they heard laughter drawing nearer and Nick and Georgie appeared in the gloom.

'What are you two lovebirds up to?' Georgie said, and David groaned softly and let Molly go—but not far.

'Just getting a little fresh air,' he said, pulling her back against him, and Nick chuckled.

'A likely story. We've been sent to find you. Mum and George are heading off soon, and she wants Molly to help her change.'

'Ah. Right. OK. We'll be with you in a minute.'

'Just mind you are—'

'Come on, Georgie, leave them to it,' Nick said diplomatically, steering her away, to David's evident relief, and letting Molly go, he stepped back and took a few deep breaths.

'Better?'

He gave a strangled laugh. 'I'll do. For now. You'd better go and help Liz change. I'll go and find Dad in a minute.'

His father was standing in the bar, surrounded by his friends, but when David appeared he broke away and came over to him.

'All right, son?'

He smiled. 'Yeah, I'm good. You?'

His father nodded, slinging an arm around his shoulder. 'Very good. Very happy.'

'She's lovely, you know. Liz. A wonderful woman. I'm so happy for you.'

'I couldn't want for more,' his father said sincerely. 'When your mother died, I never thought I'd love again, but you know there's always room for love in our lives. It's just a case of finding the way.'

'Well, you seem to have found it.'

'Indeed I have. I just hope you do, too. You've been alone too long, David. Marriage is wonderful, you should give it a try.'

He gave a short laugh. 'It's just a case of finding the right woman.'

'I rather thought you might have done that,' his father said softly, and David met his eyes briefly and looked away.

'Yeah, minor problem. I live on the other side of the world, Dad. My life's there. I live in Australia now, and I'm not coming back. How can I?'

'If it meant enough, you'd find a way,' George replied, but David didn't see how. And anyway, it was ridiculous. He hardly knew Molly. What on earth was he thinking about? He must be going crazy.

CHAPTER NINE

'WELL, I think that was a very good day.'

Georgie was sitting on the veranda with her feet up on Nick's lap, and behind him David could hear Molly in the kitchen with the children, dishing out juice and biscuits. They'd all been down on the jetty crabbing, and they'd strolled along the river wall in the sunshine, and now they were back at Molly's house relaxing.

'Today, or yesterday?' he asked his sister with a smile.

'Yesterday. Well, both, but I was talking about the wedding. I thought it was lovely.'

'It was,' he agreed. 'They both seemed really happy.'

'Did Dad talk to you about taking over the business?' Georgie asked, and he felt his smile slip.

'No. He said he was thinking of retiring, but he didn't mention that.' Probably because he'd made it clear he was staying in Australia, he thought, and wondered if he'd crushed another of his father's hopes and dreams. Just when he'd thought they were getting somewhere.

Well, so be it. There was nothing he could do about it, he didn't live here any more. He gave an inward sigh, just as Molly came back out with a tray and set it down on the table.

'Here, Georgie, your tea. Nick, your coffee.' She handed David a mug and sat down beside him with a smile that faded round the edges as she looked at him. 'Are you OK?'

'Fine, thanks,' he said, but he wasn't, not really, because it was beginning to dawn on him exactly what he'd be leaving behind, and it was getting more and more difficult to be philosophical about it.

Then Nick turned to him. 'I'd like to know a bit more about your hotels,' he said. 'We've all got lots of ideas from the other side of the desk, both on the gym and beauty spa side and also the hotel element, and we've taken on a really good manager if his references are to be believed, but running this health club is going to be a new departure for all of us and all the research in the world can't compete with experience.'

David gave a short laugh. Only last week Nick had been highly suspicious of him and ready to kill him. Now, he wanted his advice and the benefit of his experience? Whatever, David accepted it with good grace, knowing that his only real concern had been protecting Georgie, and he was with him all the way on that.

'Sure. What do you want to know?'

Nick laughed. 'If I knew that, I wouldn't have to ask. You've seen the club, you know what we've got on offer, and if it works, we're thinking of maybe building another—perhaps starting a small chain. I just wondered if you had any hints that could help make it work.'

He thought about it for a second, then shrugged. 'I think what you've done so far looks pretty good. Certainly the groundwork's all there,' he told him. 'I tell you what, I've got brochures on all the hotels in my bag. I'll get them. That'll be a good start. I can talk you through the services and the staffing and so on, and it'll make more sense if you know where I'm talking about.'

He went down to the cabin, rummaged in the bag and went back with a folder full of information on the small chain he and Cal had painstakingly built up over the last eight or nine years. He'd been meaning to show it to Molly and his father, but somehow he just hadn't got round to it.

'Wow. I didn't realise there were so many,' Georgie said, sitting up and rifling through them. 'They're all very different.'

'They are, and yet they've got a corporate identity which is recognisable,' he said, getting into his stride. 'That's important in a chain, but individuality is just as important. It needs to feel familiar but different, and you've got to work that out. Play on the strengths of each location.'

Nick nodded, and pulled out another brochure, and Georgie gasped and took it from him.

'Oh, is this the retreat?'

'Yes—there's a plan in the back, I can show you where my lodge is so you can picture me,' he said with a grin.

'I want to see you in it!' she said, and turned the pages, sighing with longing. 'Oh, I love it. Nick, can we go?'

Nick eyed her swollen abdomen and laughed. 'What, right now?'

'Idiot. Not now. In a couple of years, when we can leave the children.'

'You don't have to leave the children,' David protested, but Georgie just laughed.

'Humour me, here, David,' she said with a smile. 'I'm fantasising.'

* * *

They all laughed. All except Molly.

He'd never shown her the brochures, but as Georgie flicked through the one for the retreat, she looked over her shoulder and felt the ache inside grow.

How could he ever leave that? It was beautiful. Beautiful and remote and tranquil and exotic, quietly screaming luxury despite the apparent simplicity of it all.

Glowing wooden floors in the lodges, simple furniture, the beds draped in fine white muslin to keep out the insects so you could sleep with the walls open to the turquoise sea or the dark, mysterious rainforest.

And at night with all the lights on around the pool and dining area, it shone like a jewel—not a diamond, but amber, soft and muted and somehow hushed, with the awesome presence of the rainforest just inches away.

This was his home, she realised, and there was no way he would ever leave it. How could he? She'd always known that, but the tiny seed of hope that she'd allowed to grow was suddenly and abruptly crushed under the weight of truth.

She met his eyes, and saw the truth reflected there.

Their relationship was all an illusion—smoke and mirrors, to hide a yawning void that stretched halfway round the world…

She didn't come to him that night.

He hadn't really expected her to, because he'd seen the look in her eyes and known she'd retreat.

It was shocking how much he missed her. How much worse would it be when he went home?

He laughed softly in the darkness. Another home? That made three in the last week or two.

A light came on in the house, and he got up on his

crutches and swung over to the window, parting the curtain carefully.

Her studio—the new one, the room where she'd started to paint again. She'd been painting the day before yesterday, and she was back in there now, at one o'clock in the morning.

So she couldn't sleep either.

He pulled on his jeans and put his leg on, then went over to the house, filling the kettle and then going upstairs to her studio. She was standing with her back to him, slapping bold swathes of colour on to a blank canvas—turquoise and vivid green and the soft shadows of burnt umber. He thought she was angry at first, but then her shoulders drooped and she turned to him, and he realised she was crying.

He looked again at the canvas, and a sharp pain stabbed through him. She was painting the rainforest, he realised, seeing the brilliant red of a cassowary's head above a dark smear in the midst of the soaring greens, the flat calm of the tropical sea, the rainbow colours of the reef.

'Come here,' he said softly, and held out his arms to her, and she walked slowly towards him, the tears sliding down her cheeks with every step.

She rested her face against his chest, and the tears running down his skin were like rivers of acid, burning all the way to his heart. He folded his arms around her and held her while she cried soundlessly, awkward with her because there was nothing he could say that would change it. Wishing there was.

'Come downstairs,' he murmured, and she eased out of his arms and went down, leaving him to follow. By the time he caught up with her she had the mugs out of the cupboard and was making the tea, and they went out on to the veranda and sat staring out into the night.

'I don't suppose there's any point in asking you to come with me?' he said after an age.

She looked up at him, her eyes red-rimmed and her mouth soft and swollen. 'How?' she asked simply.

'You could let the house.'

'Only after it's finished, and that's light years away. And the house is the least of my worries.'

'So what are your worries?'

She stared at him blankly. 'What are they? Uh— Charlie?'

'Charlie would love it there.'

She rolled her eyes. 'David, how many times have I heard you say that there are no children in the retreat? It's an adults-only resort. That's the whole point of it. There's no place for Charlie there.'

'Charlie would be fine. He's a sensible boy.'

'But he needs friends. He'd have to go to school. Where's the nearest school?'

He was silent for a moment, then sighed. 'I haven't the faintest idea.'

'No, of course you haven't. The staff must live nearby, though. Where do they send their kids?'

He shifted uncomfortably. 'They all live on site. They're mostly young, single and there for the diving.'

'Right. And Cal?'

'Cal's single—well, technically. He doesn't live there, anyway. He's got a base near Port Douglas, but he rotates round the hotels.'

'And do you ever do that?'

'Oh, yes, all the time. The retreat's my base, but we've got a management suite in all the other hotels.'

'And how many of them take children?'

'Three,' he said heavily. And he didn't like any of them enough to live in them.

'Just three. Out of—how many?'

'Eleven. Well, nearly twelve. We've got one we're commissioning soon.'

She shook her head and stared out over the moonlit river. 'And it's not just that. It's what we'd be leaving behind.'

'This house?' he said, perhaps a little foolishly because she glared at him.

'It may not be up to your standards, but it's the best I could do with Robert's life insurance, and I'm getting there.'

Oh, hell. 'Molly, I'm sorry, I didn't mean it like that. I meant—it's just a house, an inanimate object. It's not—'

'What? A person? No. It's not. And I didn't mention the house, you did,' she pointed out. 'Actually, I was thinking of Robert's parents. They've already lost their son. I can't ask them to lose their grandson, too. Or my parents. They'd all be devastated.'

'They could come and stay—'

'What, once or twice a year? They're getting old. It's too far. No. It wouldn't work.'

'They could fly business class.'

'What part of no don't you understand, David?' she said, a break in her voice. 'We can't do this! It won't work. We both knew that this was only going to be—'

'Don't say fling,' he said, suddenly desperate for her not to trash what they'd had. 'Please, don't say fling.'

'I wasn't going to,' she said softly. 'It's much more

than that, at least for me. But it was only ever going to be for now, and not for ever. We both knew that.'

He sighed raggedly and scrubbed a hand through his hair. 'There's knowing, and there's knowing, though, isn't there?' he said, and she nodded.

'I'm going to miss you.'

She nodded again.

'Come to bed. Let me hold you.'

She shook her head. 'I can't. I'll just cry.'

'So cry. Maybe I'll cry, too. I just need to hold you, Molly. I need to love you.'

I do love you, he thought, and it took his breath away. In all the years since he'd first realised that girls were his for the asking, he'd never once been in danger of losing his heart. But he'd lost it now, and it hit him like a sledgehammer.

He stood up and held out his hand. 'Come with me,' he repeated, and she got up and put her hand in his and followed him to the cabin.

'When will you go?'

He turned his head and met her eyes, his own shadowed.

'I don't know. When Dad and Liz get back?'

'Right.'

So that gave her two more weeks with him, then— two more weeks of loving and aching and crying in secret, trying to be brave and all the time wanting to beg and plead with him to stay.

No. She wouldn't do that. She wouldn't beg, or plead, or grovel. And she couldn't go, so that was the end of it. She'd just be there for him, for the time he had, and take what she was offered and be grateful that she'd met him and that they'd had this short while together, like an oasis in the desert of her life.

'We'd better make the best of it, then,' she said lightly and, reaching out, she took his face in her hands and rained kisses over his eyes, his lips, the taut planes of his jaw. The stubble grazed her lips and made them tingle, ultra-sensitive now so that she was completely aware of the texture and taste of his skin, memorising it inch by inch as she moved slowly, thoroughly, over the whole of his body.

Finally he arched up, a deep groan torn from him, and rolling her over, claimed her with a single powerful thrust that took her straight over the edge. Then he cried out, the words distorted, so that she couldn't be sure if he'd really said them.

But it had sounded like, 'I love you.'

They had a few bittersweet days after that.

He finished painting the cabin, but she didn't do any more work for her exhibition. She would have all the time in the world to paint when he was gone and, for now, she just wanted to be with him. So she scraped and filled and painted, and then held the ladder, heart in her mouth, while he did the barge boards all the way up on the gable ends of the house, and when Charlie came home from school he'd take him down to the jetty and sit with him, dangling a line in the water and waiting for the little shore crabs to take the bacon rind.

They had competitions, and he didn't let Charlie win. Well, not obviously, and not always, by any means, and she loved him all the more for that.

Then they'd go back to the house and sometimes she would cook, and sometimes he would, knocking up some amazing little number with flair and lightning speed, and Charlie thought he was amazing.

Clever boy, to have worked that one out.

She was worried about him, though. He was getting too close to David, and she knew it was going to hurt him, so they talked about David going back.

'Why does he have to go?' Charlie asked one evening as she tucked him up in bed. 'Can't he live here with us?'

She shook her head, groping for words. 'He lives in Australia,' she told him. 'It's on the other side of the world.'

'I know that,' he said with all the scorn of the very young and naïve. 'But why?'

'Because it's where his hotels are,' she explained for the umpteenth time.

'Can't he have hotels here?'

'Not like the ones he's got there,' she said, seeing again in her mind the soft focus brochure of the rainforest retreat, the trees wreathed in mist, the clear turquoise water, the walls open to the elements. 'We don't have the right weather, and we aren't on the Great Barrier Reef.'

'But it's lovely here. You always tell me it's lovely. People want to come here—they stay with us and they say it's great. He could buy the pub.'

'Except it's not for sale, and it's really not the same.'

He twisted round on to his back and stared up at her earnestly. 'I know! We could go! We could go and see him.'

'Maybe,' she said, and Charlie rolled his eyes.

'You *always* say that when you mean no.'

'Perhaps one day,' she said, but she felt a flicker of hope and crushed it ruthlessly. No. They wouldn't be going. It was crazy to even think about it. Or to think about seeing him when he came back to visit his father and sister.

Her heart thumped, and she wondered if they'd have

to move, to go right away so she wouldn't be torn in two every time he came over and stirred things up.

'Anyway, what about Grannie and Grandpa?' she asked. 'They'd miss you.'

'They could come too.'

'I think they're a bit old. It's a very long way.'

'They only have to sit in a plane. They sit all day anyway. What's the difference?'

A child's logic. If only it were that straightforward.

'It isn't quite the same and, apart from anything else, it's expensive.'

His little face fell. 'Oh. That means we can't go, either, not even maybe. We never do things if they're expensive.'

She hugged him gently. 'It's not just the money, Charlie. It's all our friends and family, your cousins, your grandparents—'

'Just a holiday,' he said plaintively, but there was no point. A holiday would just bring it all back, make it hurt again, dredge up all the agony of losing David all over again.

And he hadn't even left yet...

'Is he settled?'

She sighed and nodded. 'Yes. Finally.'

'What's up?' he asked softly, reaching out and snagging her hand, tugging her over to his side. He was sitting outside on the veranda with his feet up on the rail, and she leant against him, her arms wrapped round his head, and he turned his face into the softness of her breasts, inhaling the warm, musky scent of her perfume, and felt a sharp stab of desire.

'He wants to come and visit you,' she said, and he could hear her voice was clogged with tears.

Oh, damn.

He dropped his feet to the floor and pulled her on to his lap, and she leant against his chest and propped her head against his and sighed a little unevenly. 'I wish…'

'I know.'

They didn't talk any more. There was nothing to say they hadn't said a hundred times, so he just held her, and when the sun had sunk below the horizon and the sky had turned to flame and purple and then to black, he lifted her in his arms and carried her to the cabin and made love to her with a desperation he couldn't quite conceal…

His phone rang, the ring-tone harsh and incongruous in the aftermath of their lovemaking, and he groaned and reached out, meaning to turn it off.

But it was Cal, and he understood time zones. He wouldn't be ringing for nothing, David knew, and he twisted round, swinging his legs over the side of the bed and pressing the button.

'Cal, hi. What's up?'

'We've lost your manager. His mother's dying. I'm up here at the moment, but we've got a crisis down in Port Douglas and I need to get back there. I hate to do this to you, but I know the wedding's over and I can't be in two places at once. I was just wondering if I could talk you into cutting it short.'

He felt the sands of time running away under his feet, and closed his eyes. 'Can't you get a temp in to help you out and move your manager up there for a week or so?'

'Done that. It's not working. He can't take the dive boat out and we're having difficulty filling that with any-one I'd trust.'

David swore under his breath, and Molly's hand settled gently on his shoulder.

'Go,' she said softly. 'It's time. He needs you.'

You need me, he wanted to yell. And I need you. To hell with the business.

But he didn't. He said, 'OK, mate, don't worry, I'm on my way. I'll see you soonest. I'll give you a call when I land.'

And he cut the connection, threw the phone down and shifted so he could see her face.

'Come with me,' he said roughly, hearing the tremor in his voice and hating it. 'Just to see.'

'There's no point,' she said sadly. 'It's over, David. It's been wonderful, but it's over, and it's time to let it go.'

She turned away from him, reaching for her clothes and pulling them on, and he watched her as she covered the body which had brought him so much joy in the last two weeks—the body he'd never see again.

He swallowed hard and looked away, reaching for his crutches and heading for the bathroom.

'I'll make some tea,' she said, and he nodded.

'Thanks. I'll just get dressed and phone the airport.'

So this was it. He was going. Now. Tonight.

She felt sick, but there was nothing she could do about it. He came into the kitchen as she poured the tea into the mugs, and she turned and looked at him.

'I've got a car coming in half an hour. I'm on the six o'clock flight.'

'What about Charlie?'

He swallowed hard. 'Tell him goodbye from me.'

She nodded. 'OK. Um—your tea.'

She pushed it towards him, but he didn't touch it.

Instead he held out his arms, and she went into them and stood there, feeling the hard, solid warmth of his body against hers, so familiar now, so very dear.

'Make love to me,' she whispered. 'Please? One last time.'

They went to the cabin, to the place which had become their sanctuary, and, shutting the door, he led her to the bed and undressed her swiftly. There were no preliminaries, no subtleties, no flowery words and phrases. They reached for each other in a desperate silence broken only by gasps and groans and, at last, a sob she couldn't hold down any longer, and he folded her against his chest and held her tight.

'I can hear a car,' she said at last, and he pulled on his clothes, bent and pressed a hard, swift kiss to her lips and, picking up his bags, he headed for the door.

'I've left the keys of the Saab on the chest of drawers. Can you give them to Dad, please—ask him to keep it for when I'm over here.'

She nodded. 'Go. Go on. Don't keep him waiting.'

'Say goodbye to Charlie for me.'

'I will.'

'And—thank you,' he said, his voice rough with emotion. 'Thank you for everything.'

She couldn't answer and, after a second's hesitation, he turned on his heel and left.

She heard the car door shut, then the crunch of tyres as it drove away, and then the silence of the night descended once more, suffocating her.

Or was that because a sob was wedged in her throat and she couldn't breathe?

She tried—let the breath out, sucked it in again sharply to stifle the pain, but it wouldn't stop, just kept rolling over and over her, and she curled on to her side, dragging the quilt up into her arms and clinging to it as if by holding it, holding the bedclothes which had covered him and carried his scent, she could hold him there in her heart…

CHAPTER TEN

'GOD, mate, you look rough.'

'Don't, Cal. Really. Just don't go there.'

Cal's smile faded and he looked more closely. Then, swearing softly under his breath, he took his bags from him and led him out to the chopper.

'Get in. I'll just do the checks and we're off.'

'Don't we have any guests?'

'Not on this run.'

David nodded gratefully, slid into the co-pilot's seat and buckled himself in. His throat was raw from holding down the emotion that was threatening to tear him in half, and he just wanted to get into the privacy of his lodge and be alone.

The last—absolutely the last—thing he needed was Cal interrogating him.

And maybe, for once, his old friend picked up on that, because he flew him straight to the retreat, dropped the chopper down on the helipad and unloaded his luggage without a word.

'Hi, boss!' Kelly, one of the staff called, waving to him. 'Good wedding?'

'Great, thanks,' he said, and discovered that apparently he could lie convincingly because she didn't accuse him of telling flagrant porkies, just smiled and carried on. So why did Cal have to see straight through him?

'OK, here you go. Is there anything I can get you?'

Molly?

'No, I'm good. Thanks.'

Cal gave a soft snort and headed for the door. 'I'll stick around till tomorrow. You get your head down and I'll see you for breakfast before I go.'

'You don't need to stay—'

'Yeah, I do. You look like you've been hit by a truck. I don't know what the hell's happened to you, DC, but until you look as if you aren't going to drive all the guests away, I'm going to cover you. Now get some rest, and I'll see you in the morning. There's food in your fridge if you want anything.'

And drink.

He discovered that, pulled out a beer, swallowed it in one and stripped off his clothes before heading for the shower. Then he had to find his beach leg, because he couldn't just strip off and walk into the water, because nothing was that easy.

He wanted to cry—to howl, to rant, to scream with the pain, but he'd learned over the last three years to deal with that, and this was very little different. So he picked up a towel and went out on to the veranda, turned on the taps, and with the rainforest closing quietly round him like a mother's arms, he turned his face up to the water and let the silent, scalding tears fall at last.

'Welcome back, boss.'

'Good to have you home.'

'Nice to see you, DC.'

'How was the wedding?'

'How's your dad?'

'Have a good holiday?'

How many more of them were there? He didn't know how long he could go on being polite, and he had no idea where Cal was. Not in his lodge, anyway. The office, probably. He headed up there, and found him on the phone.

He lifted a finger, ended the call and swung his feet to the ground. 'How're you doing?'

There was no polite way to describe it, so he didn't bother to be polite, and Cal just laughed.

'Come on, you need caffeine and calories. We'll take something out on the boat.'

'There's no need.'

'Yeah, there is. I want to know what's going on, and you're going to tell me if I have to drag it out of you.'

'You nag worse than Molly,' he said, his voice cracking on her name, and Cal shot him a keen look, swore and ushered him out the back way to the boathouse. They passed Kelly, and Cal snapped an order at her and propelled him down the path to the boats. They'd just cast off and were heading out to the end of the jetty when she reappeared with a basket.

'Coffee and pastries. Have a nice breakfast!' she said cheerfully, and Cal opened up the throttle and took them out into the middle of the bay before cutting the engine and letting the boat drift.

'Molly, eh?'

David stared out over the bay and swallowed hard. 'She's a friend of Liz's—my father's new wife. I stayed with her.'

Cal blinked. 'So—she's—what? Fifties?'

'No. Hell, no, she's about thirty, thirty-one? I don't know exactly. We didn't talk about her date of birth.'

'Single?'

'Widow. With a boy. Charlie. He's eight.'

His throat closed up again, and he reached for the coffee Cal was handing him.

'So—you fell in love.'

'Is it so obvious?'

'Oh, yeah. To me. Kelly wouldn't notice. She's lost her contacts.'

He laughed at that. 'And the others?'

'They probably just think you've been partying too hard. Anyway, they're used to you looking rough.'

'Well, cheers, I feel so much better.'

Cal chuckled, then lifted his head and studied him closely. 'So—since you look as if she's stolen all the toys out of your pram, I take it this is the real thing?'

He stared down into the coffee. 'No. No, it was always going to be just a short-lived thing. We both knew that.'

'Did your heart know? Because it looks like you kept that one a secret.'

He sighed. 'She just—got under my skin, you know? I didn't mean to fall—' He broke off, looking away and clamping down on that surge of pain until it was back in control. 'I've never been in love, Cal,' he confessed softly. 'I didn't realise it could hurt like this.'

'You should have asked me. It's a bummer.'

'Tell me about it.'

'And what does Molly think of you being in love with her?'

'Molly doesn't know.'

'Oh, ace. And is she in love with you?'

He shrugged. 'She didn't say. But she wouldn't come.

She says she has to stay in England for Charlie's grand-parents. They've lost their son. She says that's enough.'

'That's a tough one. I can see her point.'

'So can I. That's the trouble.'

'Of course if she knew you loved her—'

'It wouldn't change the facts.'

Cal sighed thoughtfully, and for a moment they were both silent. Then he went on, 'And your father? How's he?'

'Oh, he's good. Really happy. Except he wants to retire, and Georgie thought he was going to ask me to take over the business.'

'I take it you pointed out that you're a little tied up already?'

He smiled bleakly. 'Oh, yes. It went down like a lead balloon. They want me to move back for good.'

Cal grinned. 'Well, you know, any time you want to hand over your side of the business, DC, I'm more than happy to talk terms.'

David snorted. 'You couldn't even manage a staffing crisis without me,' he pointed out, and Cal grunted.

'It was just Murphy's law. I would have managed.'

Then why couldn't you? he wanted to say, but he didn't, because it wouldn't have got any better if he'd stayed longer, and it probably would have been worse.

Although how, frankly, he found it hard to imagine.

'So—enough about me. Fill me in on what's been going on,' he said, and tried very hard to concentrate.

'So how's the exhibition stuff going?'

Molly shrugged. 'Rubbish. It's odd. I keep painting, but nothing that I was working on before seems to say anything to me, and the new ones—I can't show them, Liz. They're—' Different. Scarily so.

'May I see?'

She hesitated for a moment, then shrugged again. 'Sure. Why not?'

She led Liz up to her studio and opened the door, and she gasped.

'Oh—Molly! Oh, Molly, they're incredible!' she breathed.

She lifted her shoulders helplessly. 'I can't seem to paint anything else.'

'But—they're wonderful. You've really captured him.'

'Rather personal, though.'

They were. He was naked in many of them, but she didn't paint so figuratively that they were explicitly revealing. She'd used her familiar technique of broken images and overlays, so he was suggested rather than drawn exactly but, nevertheless, the mood, the atmosphere was intensely private, raw sensuality radiating from the images almost tangibly.

They frightened Molly they were so intense, but she couldn't seem to paint him any other way.

'Has Georgie seen them?'

She shook her head. 'No. I didn't know if she should see her brother like that. They're a bit—'

'They are—but they're beautiful. Striking.'

'But I have to earn a living, and I can't sell these. It would be like selling him—'

She bit her lip and, with a gentle sigh, Liz took her into her arms and rocked her like a baby.

'I miss him,' she said through her tears, and Liz's arms tightened.

'I know you do, my love.'

'It's so silly,' she said, easing away and walking to the window so she could stare down at the cabin. She spent hours doing that, pretending he was still in there, or else going in there herself and lying on the bed huddled in his dirty sheets which she still couldn't bring herself to wash.

'Why is it silly? You love him,' Liz said softly, and she pressed her fist to her mouth to stop the howl of pain from coming out.

'You know, it's worse than losing Robert,' she told her, turning her back on the cabin and meeting Liz's caring eyes. 'When he died, I knew he was gone, and there was nothing I could do about it, but this—this is so much worse, because he is alive, and we could be together if only it wasn't all so hard—'

'He misses you.'

Her head came up again, and she searched Liz's face eagerly. 'Did he say so?'

'No—not in so many words, but your father says he sounds lost. He won't talk for long, and he won't talk to me, and George is worried about him. And you. He really hoped you'd find a way to be together.'

She wrapped her arms around her waist, holding herself together. She seemed to spend most of the day like that, fighting the pain and the nausea, and then at night she'd paint, furiously throwing colour at the canvas until she fell into bed exhausted before dawn.

There was one picture of him as she imagined him in the shower, water streaming over him with the rain-forest as backdrop, another with him sitting on the end of the jetty, one leg hitched up, fishing. In one he was laughing, his head thrown back, the sheer joy of living radiating off him.

Then there were the pensive ones, sitting on the jetty staring out over the water, standing in the forest with the trees towering above him, walking away from her on the beach.

And then there were the intimate ones, the ones of him as only she had seen him, his eyes smouldering with passion.

'I can't show these,' she said, and Liz nodded.

'No. It wouldn't be fair. But you needed to paint them.'

'I never painted Robert like that.'

Liz didn't reply. Hard to find the right words, Molly thought. She couldn't.

'How's Charlie?'

'Sad. Lonely. He really, really misses him. I thought—it wasn't long enough for us to all feel so much, you know? Not this much. And I can't begin to explain to him why it all hurts so badly.'

She bit her lip and met Liz's eyes. 'Do you think we should go to him? I mean, it would be the logical thing, because of his business. I can paint anywhere, and Charlie's too young for his schooling to be disrupted, and anyway, he's so unhappy, but his grandparents... I don't know what to do, Liz. I just know I'll never get over him, but I can't keep painting him for ever. I have to earn a living.'

'So exhibit these.'

She felt shocked. 'No! No, I can't. It would be wrong.'

'No. It would be very personal, but they're the best thing you've ever done, and you'd be a fool to yourself if you didn't show them. They're so compelling.'

She stared at them. 'Really?'

'Really. And you need to put your prices up. A lot. Ask Georgie and Nick. They like art. And Daniel. He's a bit of a collector, too. Get their opinion.'

So she did, and they all told her she'd be crazy not

to exhibit them. But there were some she held back, some that were too personal for her to allow even Liz to see. Ones where she'd looked into his eyes and seen right down to his soul…

She resisted, though, when they tried to get her to put them in a London gallery, so Daniel strong-armed the gallery where she was due to exhibit into hiking the prices and pushing her with an advertising campaign.

And then it was time, and she put on her beaded dress and went to the private view with George and Liz at her side, and she was stunned by the reaction. And by the number of red stickers on pictures. That would mean they were sold, but—

'There are so many red dots,' she said, dazed. 'I can't believe it—they can't all be sold.'

'Of course they can, they're fantastic,' Georgie told her, hugging her with tears in her eyes. 'You've really made him come alive. Thank you.'

But all she could think was that there would be enough money for her to go to him, to see if there was any way, any place that they could be together, because without him she was just a hollow, empty shell.

It was hot in Cairns.

Hot, and sticky, and she was so tired she didn't know what she was doing. If she did, she probably wouldn't be here, she acknowledged, but with shaking fingers she made herself dial the number she'd got from Georgie.

'Hello, the Rainforest Retreat, what can I do for you?'

It wasn't him.

She hadn't even thought beyond this point, and now she was stumped.

'Hello? Can I help you?'

'Um—hello. I'm trying to contact David Cauldwell—'

'Oh, he's out on the dive boat at the moment. Can I take your number and get him to call you?'

She didn't know who she was speaking to, but it was a man's voice so she had a stab. 'Is that Cal?'

'Yes, it is—is that Molly?' he asked, and she thought he sounded stunned.

'Oh. Yes. How do you know my name?' she asked, and there was a strangled laugh at the other end.

'Well, you're all he's talked about since he got back, so that might have something to do with it—where are you? Give me your number, or does he have it?'

She stared at the payphone. 'Um—I'm in Cairns airport—'

'Cairns?' he exclaimed, and she heard a chair scrape back. 'Stay right there, sweetheart, and I'll come and get you. You go and get yourself a drink and something to eat, and I'll be there.'

The phone went dead, and she stared at it for a second before putting it down with trembling fingers.

Cal was coming, and he was going to take her to David. Today. Now. Shortly.

Covering her mouth with her hand, she ran to the loo and lost the pitiful amount of airline food she'd managed to squeeze down over the last few hours.

Ridiculous, she thought, staring at herself in the mirror over the basin. She was white as a sheet, she'd lost loads of weight and she looked dreadful. And she was so *nervous*! Her palms were sweating, and she scrubbed them down her trousers and closed her eyes.

Go and get a drink, she told herself. Iced water, and something fruity, perhaps.

Or perhaps not.

'Great day, David! Thank you!'

'My pleasure, Doug. Have a good evening.'

His wife smiled. 'We will. That was fabulous. Thanks.'

She leant over and kissed his cheek as he helped her out of the boat, then, as he was about to put it back in the boathouse and check over the equipment, he looked up and caught sight of a woman standing on the jetty, and his heart all but stopped.

Crazy. He had to stop thinking every woman he saw was—

'Molly?'

Hell, his legs were going to give way. He started walking, then she smiled, and he started to run, until at last he reached her, sweeping her up into his arms and crushing her hard against him, choked with emotion.

Until he lifted his head and caught sight of her close to. Then he stared down at her and shook his head, fear swamping him. 'Molly, you look dreadful. What's the matter? What's happened?'

'Nothing. I lost you,' she said, and tears welled in her eyes.

And in his.

He wrapped her close again, shocked at how thin she was, stunned at the joy that was flowing through him just from holding her, touching her, being near her again after all this time.

'Come on, let's get out of here, go somewhere private,' he said gruffly and, taking her by the hand, he led her along the path to his lodge, up the steps and in, kicking the door shut and dragging her back into his arms.

His lips found hers and clung, and it was an age before either of them moved. 'Has Cal been looking after you? Have you eaten? Why didn't you tell me you were coming? I could have been there to meet you—'

She put a finger over his lips and smiled. 'Yes, no, and because I didn't know what to say.'

He shook his head, lost. He couldn't remember what he'd asked, really. 'Say about what?'

'Us,' she said simply. 'I can't live without you. I thought I'd die when Robert died, but this is far worse because it's all so unnecessary. I had to see if we could find a way to be together, because without you life just isn't worth living, and Charlie's miserable all the time. He misses you so much, and so do I. So I wanted to see if there was a way we could live here with you some of the time, maybe in the school holidays, or perhaps during the term so we can be at home in the holidays just catching up with family. Or just somehow…'

She gave a pathetic little shrug that tore at his heart-strings. 'I didn't know, but I thought—I had to try. I hoped you'd understand, hoped you wouldn't mind—'

'Mind?' He laughed a little hysterically and hugged her tight again. 'Of course I don't mind! I can't tell you how much I've missed you—'

He broke off, because he simply couldn't speak any more, and taking her dear, beloved, tearstained face in his hands, he touched his lips to hers, so carefully, so gently, as if by doing so he could tell her how much he cherished her, how barren his life had been without her.

'I need to get this wetsuit off and have a shower,' he said after an age. 'Come with me.'

'On your veranda?'

He nodded, and she smiled. 'I'd love to.'

It was just as she'd imagined it.

Eerily, uncannily so. The rainforest was so close she could reach out and touch it. Literally. And the water was cool and sweet and refreshing, and he was there, his body just as she'd remembered except thinner, like hers, because, like her, she guessed, he'd been struggling to eat.

'Come here,' he said, and she went to him and stood under the streaming water and lifted her face to his and laughed with joy.

'I have something to tell you.'

'I've got something to tell you, too—well, to show you, really, and I hope you won't be cross, because it's what got me here. Do you want to go first?'

'OK. I've sold out to Cal.'

She sat bolt upright, shocked. 'What?'

'Well, not quite like that,' he explained, pulling her back down beside him and wrapping her in his arms. 'I've sold certain parts of the business, handed over the responsibility, so I can take a backseat. He can't afford to buy me out, but he's freed up enough capital so I can do what I want.'

'Which is?' she asked, her heart pounding.

'To come home and take over from my father and go into business with Nick and Dan and Harry. And marry you. If you'll have me. If you'll marry me, and let me look after you and Charlie, and wage war on your garden and keep the drainpipes up and the roses pruned and the gates swinging on their hinges—'

'You want to live in my house? After this place?'

He laughed softly. 'It's a hotel, Molly. I thought I loved it, but it's just a business. It's where I work. It isn't home. Home is wherever you are, because I love you—'

'You love me?'

'Well, of course I love you!'

'You didn't say! I wasn't sure what you wanted, when you asked me to come out here. I thought—I don't know what I thought. That you just wanted to keep it going for a while, get me to visit you from time to time in between your trips home—I didn't realise you loved me.'

'Love you. Not loved. Love. Would it have made a difference?'

She shook her head. 'No, not really. Not until I realised that Charlie loves you, too, and that changed everything. I could make sacrifices myself, for him, but if it was hurting him, it all seemed so silly and unnecessary. The world really isn't that big, and the most important thing in it apart from Charlie is you. And I want us to be together.'

'Is that a yes, then?'

'What?'

He gave a twisted little smile. 'I asked you to marry me. I wondered if that was a yes—'

'Well, of course it's a yes!' she said, tears welling again, and his arms closed round her and wrapped her against his heart.

'Thank God,' he whispered and, turning his head, he found her lips and kissed her as if he'd never let her go.

But he did, in the end, and she told him about her exhibition. 'I hope you'll forgive me. Some of them were pretty frank. I've got a CD with them on to show you. I suppose I should have asked before I sold them.'

'I've seen them,' he said. 'Nick sent me photos.'

'He didn't say!'

His smile was slow and teasing. 'There's a lot my brother-in-law hasn't told you. I bought some of them.'

'You did?' she said, aghast. 'But—why?'

'Because he said you loved them and didn't really want to part with them. And because they're amazing, and I'm so proud of you. And because I wanted something that reminded me of you. Just in case you wouldn't let me come back.'

'Oh, David—there was never any danger I wouldn't let you come back. I need you so much. I felt as if I couldn't breathe without you there. And I've been so sick with loneliness and missing you.'

'Sick?'

She nodded. 'Every day.'

He studied her for a moment, then gave a funny little laugh and said, 'I don't suppose you've done a pregnancy test?'

'A pr—?' She stared at him blankly, then her hand flew up and covered her mouth. 'But—how—?'

'The last time—when the car was on its way to get me. I'd packed. We didn't even think of it. It didn't occur to me until later.' He tipped his head on one side. 'When was your last period?'

'My last—?'

She broke off, thinking back, trying to work out when she'd last had a period. She'd been so stressed and unhappy since he left she hadn't even thought about it, but now she did, she realised it was ages ago. Just before he arrived, she thought, but her cycle was long, nearly five weeks. And that last night would have been perfect...

She felt the smile start in her toes and work its way all the way up to her eyes. 'Oh, David. A baby—'

But then she thought of something and panicked. 'What about flying? What if I've done something dreadful to the baby—'

'It's safe,' he said. 'It's the end, I think, when it's a problem. But, just to be on the safe side, we'll go home first class so you can lie down on a proper bed and rest.'

She stared at him. 'I don't have a first class ticket.'

'Nor do I. We'll change them. I was travelling business class—'

'What do you mean, you were travelling business class?'

'I was coming home to you tomorrow,' he said softly. 'But, since you're here, we might as well spend a few days together and then go. Especially since you're in a delicate condition.'

'We don't know that,' she began, but she did, now she'd stopped grieving for him and could listen to her body. And it was telling her, without doubt, that she was carrying their baby.

She snuggled back into his arms. 'First class sounds good,' she said. 'And so does a few more days. So what are you going to do with me until then?'

He spoiled her.

He took her sailing, and snorkelling, and for walks through the rainforest, and he fed her gorgeous meals carefully designed to nourish her and not trigger the sickness, and then at the end of the week they said goodbye to Cal and flew home to Charlie.

He was staying with Nick and Georgie, but when they got back the house was deserted, so they went round to George's house and found everyone there.

Well, everyone except Nick and Georgie.

They walked in and Charlie caught sight of her first.

'Hey, Mummy!' he shrieked, and ran over to her. 'Guess what? Georgie's had her baby, and it's a boy! Did you have a nice time? Come and see the pictures of the baby—'

And then he broke off, because his eyes had swivelled to David, and his jaw dropped and he stopped dead.

'David?' he said, and then he ran, his legs flying, and threw himself at David's chest.

'Hello, sport,' he said gruffly, catching him and hugging him tight.

'I told Mummy you'd come back,' he said, his face buried in David's neck. 'She wouldn't believe me, but I knew you'd come back.'

His father was staring at him, his eyes hopeful, and he smiled and nodded.

'You were right,' he told his father. 'If something matters enough, you find a way. And I'm coming home. Hopefully taking over from you and going into business with you guys, if you're interested in that,' he added to Daniel and Harry.

And, holding out his arm to her, he drew Molly in to his side and bent his head and kissed her.

'And we're getting married,' she said.

Charlie turned his face up to David's and said, 'So will you be my daddy?'

She saw his throat work, and he bent and kissed Charlie's cheek. 'If you'll have me.'

'Can we go crabbing lots?'

David chuckled. 'Lots.'

'Cool. Are you going to have a baby?'

'Charlie, you can't ask them that, it's not polite,' George said quickly, but David smiled.

They exchanged glances, and Molly felt herself blushing.

'Well, it's funny you should mention that,' he said to his father. 'About all these grandchildren you wanted…'

* * * * *

Here's a sneak peek at
THE CEO'S CHRISTMAS PROPOSITION,
the first in USA TODAY *bestselling author*
Merline Lovelace's HOLIDAYS ABROAD *trilogy*
coming in November 2008.

American Devon McShay is about to get the
Christmas surprise of a lifetime when she meets
her new client, sexy billionaire Caleb Logan, for
the very first time.

Silhouette®

Desire

Available November 2008

Her breath whistled out in a sigh of relief when he exited Customs. Devon recognized him right away from the newspaper and magazine articles her friend and partner Sabrina had looked up during her frantic prep work.

Caleb John Logan, Jr. Thirty-one. Six-two. With jet-black hair, laser-blue eyes and a linebacker's shoulders under his charcoal-gray cashmere overcoat. His jaw-dropping good looks didn't score him any points with Devon. She'd learned the hard way not to trust handsome heartbreakers like Cal Logan.

But he was a client. An important one. And she was willing to give someone who'd served a hitch in the marines before earning a B.S. from the University of Oregon, an MBA from Stanford and his first million at the ripe old age of twenty-six the benefit of the doubt.

Right up until he spotted the hot-pink pashmina, that is.

Devon knew the flash of color was more visible than the sign she held up with his name on it. So she wasn't surprised when Logan picked her out of the crowd and cut in her direction. She'd just plastered on her best businesswoman smile when he whipped an arm around her waist. The next moment she was sprawled against his cashmere-covered chest.

"Hello, brown eyes."

Swooping down, he covered her mouth with his.

Sheer astonishment kept Devon rooted to the spot for a few seconds while her mind whirled chaotically. Her first thought was that her client had downed a few too many drinks during the long flight. Her second, that he'd mistaken the kind of escort and consulting services her company provided. Her third shoved everything else out of her head.

The man could kiss!

His mouth moved over hers with a skill that ignited sparks at a half dozen flash points throughout her body. Devon hadn't experienced that kind of spontaneous combustion in a while. A *long* while.

The sparks were still popping when she pushed off his chest, only now they fueled a flush of anger.

"Do you always greet women you don't know with a lip-lock, Mr. Logan?"

A smile crinkled the skin at the corners of his eyes. "As a matter of fact, I don't. That was from Don."

"Huh?"

"He said he owed you one from New Year's Eve two years ago and made me promise to deliver it."

She stared up at him in total incomprehension. Logan hooked a brow and attempted to prompt a non-existent memory.

"He abandoned you at the Waldorf. Five minutes before midnight. To deliver twins."

"I don't have a clue who or what you're..."

Understanding burst like a water balloon.

"Wait a sec. Are you talking about Sabrina's old boyfriend? Your buddy, who's now an ob-gyn doc?"

It was Logan's turn to look startled. He recovered faster than Devon had, though. His smile widened into a rueful grin.

"I take it you're not Sabrina Russo."

"No, Mr. Logan, I am *not*."

* * * * *

Be sure to look for
THE CEO'S CHRISTMAS PROPOSITION
by Merline Lovelace.
Available in November 2008
wherever books are sold,
including most bookstores, supermarkets,
drugstores and discount stores.

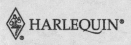
LAURA MARIE ALTOM

A Daddy for Christmas

THE STATE OF PARENTHOOD

Single mom Jesse Cummings is struggling
to run her Oklahoma ranch and raise her
two little girls after the death of her husband.
Then on Christmas Eve, a miracle strolls onto
her land in the form of tall, handsome bull
rider Gage Moore. He doesn't plan on staying,
but in the season of miracles, anything
can happen....

***Available November
wherever books are sold.***

LOVE, HOME & HAPPINESS

nocturne™

ESCAPE THE CHILL OF WINTER WITH TWO SPECIAL STORIES FROM BESTSELLING AUTHORS

MICHELE HAUF

AND

VIVI ANNA

———

WINTER KISSED

In "A Kiss of Frost," photographer Kate Wilson experiences the icy kisses of Jal Frosti, but soon learns that this icy god has a deadly ulterior motive. Can Kate's love melt his heart?

In "Ice Bound," Dr. Darien Calder travels to the north island of Japan, where he discovers an icy goddess who is rumored to freeze doomed travelers. Darien is determined to melt her beautiful but frosty exterior and break her of the curse she carries...before it's too late.

Available November wherever books are sold.

www.eHarlequin.com
www.paranormalromanceblog.wordpress.com

Romantic
SUSPENSE

Sparked by Danger, Fueled by Passion.

Lindsay McKenna
Susan Grant

Mission: Christmas

Celebrate the holidays with a pair
of military heroines and their daring men
in two romantic, adventurous stories
from these bestselling authors.

Featuring:

"The Christmas Wild Bunch"
by *USA TODAY* bestselling author
Lindsay McKenna

and

"Snowbound with a Prince"
by *New York Times* bestselling author
Susan Grant

Available November wherever books are sold.

REQUEST YOUR FREE BOOKS!
2 FREE NOVELS PLUS 2
FREE GIFTS!

H A R L E Q U I N   R O M A N C E®

From the Heart, For the Heart

Inside ROMANCE

Stay up-to-date on all your romance reading news!

The Inside Romance newsletter is a FREE quarterly newsletter highlighting our upcoming series releases and promotions!

Click on the <u>Inside Romance</u> link on the front page of **www.eHarlequin.com** or e-mail us at insideromance@harlequin.ca to sign up to receive your FREE newsletter today!

You can also subscribe by writing us at: HARLEQUIN BOOKS Attention: Customer Service Department P.O. Box 9057, Buffalo, NY 14269-9057

Please allow 4-6 weeks for delivery of the first issue by mail.

IRNBPA208

Coming Next Month

**Get into the holiday spirit this month
as Harlequin Romance® brings you...**

#4057 HER MILLIONAIRE, HIS MIRACLE Myrna Mackenzie
Heart to Heart

Rich and powerful Jeremy has just discovered he's going blind, and he's determined to keep his independence. Shy Eden has loved Jeremy from afar for so long. Can the woman he once overlooked persuade him to accept her help—and her love?

#4058 WEDDED IN A WHIRLWIND Liz Fielding

Miranda is on a dream tropical-island holiday when disaster strikes! She's trapped in a dark cave and is scared for her life...but worse, she's not alone! Miranda is trapped with macho adventurer Nick—and the real adventure is just about to begin....

#4059 RESCUED BY THE MAGIC OF CHRISTMAS
Melissa McClone

Carly hasn't celebrated Christmas for six years—not since her fiancé died. But this year, courageous mountain rescuer Jake is determined she'll enjoy herself and dispel her fear of loving again with the magic of Christmas.

#4060 BLIND DATE WITH THE BOSS Barbara Hannay
9 to 5

Sally has come to Sydney for a fresh start. And she's trying to ignore her attraction to brooding M.D. Logan. But when he's roped into attending a charity ball, fun-loving Sally waltzes into his life, and it will never be the same again....

#4061 THE TYCOON'S CHRISTMAS PROPOSAL Jackie Braun

With the dreaded holidays approaching, the last thing widowed businessman Dawson needs is a personal shopper who wants to get *personal*. But Eve is intent on getting him into the Christmas spirit, and she's hoping he'll give her the best Christmas present of all—a proposal!

#4062 CHRISTMAS WISHES, MISTLETOE KISSES Fiona Harper

After leaving her cheating husband, Louise is determined to make this Christmas perfect for her and her young son. But it's not until she meets gorgeous architect Ben that her Christmas really begins to sparkle....

HRCNM1008